Into Thin Air

The stolen plane reached one end of the runway just as the three teens reached the other. The Hardys and Jamal dashed down the worn concrete toward the oncoming plane. The plane accelerated, its engine roaring and its central prop spinning into a nearly invisible blur.

The three teens waved their arms and shouted, trying to get the plane to stop, but it merely picked up speed. The darkness made it impossible to see who was behind the controls.

"They're not slowing down!" Joe said.

"Look out!" Frank cried.

The Hardy Boys Mystery Stories™

Available from ALADDIN Paperbacks

THE **HARDY BOYS**®

#176
IN PLANE SIGHT

FRANKLIN W. DIXON

Aladdin Paperbacks

New York London Toronto Sydney Singapore

First Aladdin Paperbacks edition December 2002

Copyright © 2002 by Simon & Schuster, Inc.

ALADDIN PAPERBACKS
An imprint of Simon & Schuster
Children's Publishing Division
1230 Avenue of the Americas
New York, NY 10020

The text of this book was set in New Caledonia.

Printed in the United States of America
2 4 6 8 10 9 7 5 3

THE HARDY BOYS MYSTERY STORIES is a trademark of Simon & Schuster, Inc.

THE HARDY BOYS and colophon are registered trademarks of Simon & Schuster, Inc.

Library of Congress Control Number 2002101535

ISBN 0-7434-3760-8

Contents

IN PLANE SIGHT

1 Fly By & Buy

"Joe, I think it's time you flew this bird solo," Jamal Hawkins said, a broad smile breaking over his chestnut brown face.

Joe Hardy, a muscular seventeen-year-old with blond hair and blue eyes, took a deep breath and wiped the sweat from his palms. He reached forward and wrapped his hands around the steering yobe in front of his copilot's seat.

Jamal took his hands off the pilot's yobe and sat back. Joe turned the steering column to the right, and the Cessna dipped into a gentle starboard turn.

The single-engine four-seat Cessna 182 was part of a small fleet of planes owned by Jamal's father, Ben Hawkins, the president of Hawkins Air Service. It was an old plane, but it sported a fresh coat

1

of ivory paint with the traditional green-and-gold Hawkins Air logo and trim. It could comfortably seat four and had extra cargo room behind the rear seats.

"How's it feel, Joe?" Frank asked, leaning over from the rear of the plane. The elder of the two brothers at age eighteen, Frank was tall and lean with brown hair and eyes and the physique of a track star.

"Feels like a million bucks," Joe replied, beaming.

"Believe me," Jamal said, "it's not the plane that feels that way. It's your new pilot's license!"

"I'm glad the prize we got from the Halloween Spooktacular contest allowed you to finish up your certification, Joe," Frank said. "The brushup course I took didn't hurt either."

"It seems like ages since either of us has flown a plane," Joe said. He gazed through the blur of the prop into the cloudy sky beyond. The brothers' busy schedules at Bayport High didn't leave them much time for flying, even though Jamal's dad owned an air taxi company.

"It hasn't been *that* long," Frank replied, "but I do feel a little rusty." He smiled. "Remind your dad to have out-of-town business more often. It's nice to have a chance to stretch our wings, so to speak."

Jamal nodded. "I'm glad he trusted me to do this," he said. "We were lucky that this flying show fell on a teachers' conference weekend for both our schools." Even though Jamal attended a different

2

high school from the brothers, the three of them were good friends. They often competed against one another in sporting events.

"Thanks for asking us to come along," Frank said. "I've read about the Fly By & Buy air show before and always wanted to check it out."

"No problem," Jamal replied. "With you guys, I get three things: copilots, someone to help me pick up this new plane for Dad, and someone to hang with during the show. Most of the people who come to these things are my dad's age. How's our heading, Joe?"

Joe checked the instruments and turned the plane slightly to the north. "Headed straight for the old Scott airstrip," he replied. The airport was outside Jewel Ridge, a town a couple of hours north of Bayport. "Kind of a strange place to hold an air show, isn't it?"

"A strange time of year, too," Frank said. "I saw on the news that there's already snow on the ground in the state park north of there, and most of the lakes are frozen over."

Jamal shrugged. "Maybe they got a price break for using the airport this weekend. The show was earlier last year, and the year before too. I read in the paper that Fly By & Buy was having some kind of financial trouble. That's why they moved the show location out into the sticks, where it's cheaper."

"There can't be a lot of competing shows this

time of year either," Joe said. "I imagine most of these small airports are pretty empty right now." He made another small adjustment, and the plane dipped to starboard.

"Well, Scott Field won't be empty this weekend," Jamal said. "Fly By & Buy always attracts a good crowd: lots of experimental aircraft, lots of collectors. Not many women our age, though." He threw a sly grin toward the Hardys.

"Joe and I are spoken for, so that's all right," Frank replied.

"I thought you were still going out with Vanessa Robinson anyway," Joe said to Jamal.

"We're dating," Jamal said, "but we're not tied to each other. You know how college girls can be."

Joe and Frank glanced at each other and shrugged. They'd been dating Iola Morton and Callie Shaw for a *long* time.

"Okay, so maybe you *don't* know," Jamal said good-naturedly.

The three teens laughed.

"So," Frank said, "tell us about this airplane we're picking up."

"It's an old Sullivan Brothers Air Customizing job," Jamal replied. "Pretty sleek—and pretty expensive, too, though Dad got a good deal on it. It's based on a Cessna Caravan and seats eight. It also comes with some sweet appointments inside. Dad hopes it'll beef up our high-end business."

4

"That model's sometimes used for cargo and military expeditions, isn't it?" Joe asked.

"Yeah," Jamal said, "but not these Sullivan babies. They're too posh for that. Some of 'em are real collectors' items."

"I can't wait to see it," Frank said.

"I can't wait to *fly* it," Jamal replied, leaning contentedly back in the pilot's seat and smiling.

The Cessna's single engine hummed confidently as they plowed through the clouds toward their destination.

Frank reached down and checked the two parachutes stowed beneath his seat.

"Worried about your brother's flying?" Jamal asked, smiling.

"Nah, just checking," Frank said. "I really hope we have a chance to do some jumps while we're here," he said, changing the subject.

"If the weather stays good," Jamal said, "I'm sure someone will be taking parachutists up. I'd take you myself, but Dad would probably kill me—for insurance reasons, of course."

"You jeopardize his insurance, so he collects on yours," Joe replied with a smile. "Seems reasonable."

The scenery below the plane grew progressively more hilly as they moved away from Bayport and toward Jewel Ridge. It was a pretty flight, though the foliage had mostly passed its autumn peak. The afternoon sunlight glittered off the Jewel River, which wound upstream toward the small city and their destination. It had been unseasonably warm lately, so the river remained unfrozen. Patches of snow huddled in the shadows of the hills and bare forests below, though, reminding the Hardys of the colder weather they'd been having.

Jamal took the controls again. They passed west of the city, angling toward Scott Field.

The old airstrip stood alone amid gently rolling hills, not too far from the village of Scottsville on Jewel Ridge's northwestern outskirts. The airfield had a small old-fashioned control tower, about three stories tall, with a walkway around the upper deck. A long row of tubular metal airplane hangars lined the edge of the field nearest the main road. An L-shaped brick administration building stood nearby, and a row of service buildings ran behind the hangars.

The airport's three runways were laid out in a traditional triangular design, aligned with the prevailing winds to allow for the best takeoffs and landings. Close to the end of the runway farthest from the hangars was another long, boxy building with what looked like a small park next to it. A dusty road circled the west side of the airport and led to a smaller complex.

"That's the old Flyboy Motel," Jamal said, "and the campground beside it. Are you guys *sure* you don't want to spring for rooms? It could get pretty cold tonight."

"Is Hawkins Air picking up the bill?" Joe asked, arching an eyebrow.

"Well . . ." Jamal began.

"A little cold-weather camping is good for the soul," Frank said with a laugh.

"And the wallet too, I guess," Jamal admitted.

"That little motel is probably booked solid for the show anyway," Joe said. He scanned the rows of aircraft assembled by the edges of the field, just off the runways. Many different types of planes stood side by side: single engines, twin engines, a few small jets, and a variety of strange-looking experimental and home-built aircraft. Most had been buffed to sparkling finishes. "The organizers may have changed the date of the Fly By & Buy," he added, "but it looks like they've still got good attendance."

"Usually it's the largest show in this part of the country," Frank said. "A lot of important local air business goes on here."

"Even more, now that *we've* arrived," Jamal said. "Check your seat belts; I'm taking us down."

Jamal radioed the control tower for permission to land. Once he had a runway, he vectored in from the southeast and brought them smoothly down to the ground.

After taxiing to their assigned parking area, the teens gathered their luggage and hopped out of the plane.

"Looks like the Jewel Ridge economic boom

7

hasn't drifted this far north yet," Frank noted, eyeing the weeds growing around the edges of the patchy-looking tarmac.

"There's a busier airport just south of town," Jamal said. "I flew in there with Dad once."

"Busier, but not friendlier," said a woman's voice from behind them.

The three friends turned and saw a tall red-haired woman walking toward them. She was dressed in a natty maroon business suit and high heels, which looked impractical on the tarmac's rough surface. She was smiling brightly.

"I'm Elise Flaubert," she said, "director of the Scottsville Airport and the show coordinator. Which one of you is Jamal Hawkins?"

"The tall, dark, and handsome one," Joe said.

"The *other* tall, dark, and handsome one," Frank added, smiling.

Elise Flaubert laughed and extended her hand to Jamal. She shook his hand and then shook hands with the brothers as well.

"Frank and Joe Hardy," Frank said. "We're attending the show with Jamal."

"I'm keeping them out of trouble," Jamal said.

Ms. Flaubert frowned slightly, then seemed to decide Jamal was joking and smiled again. "Are you related to the famous detective Fenton Hardy?" she asked the brothers.

"He's our father," Joe replied.

"Ah. I've heard a lot about him," Ms. Flaubert said. "Well, Mr. Hawkins, I think you'll be happy with this show." She handed him a manila envelope. "You'll find the show information and your ID badges inside. If you need anything else, just ask." She sighed and glanced at her watch. "Shoot! Look at the time. Got to go!"

With that, she bustled back across the aging tarmac toward a man picking up litter. "Jose," she said, her voice fading into the distance, "aren't you supposed to be working the cafeteria right now . . . ?"

"Friendly," Joe observed, "but harried."

"You want to check in at the campground?" Frank asked.

"Let's look around a little first," Jamal replied, looking over the rows of planes lining the field. "Hey, check out that baby!"

He walked toward a bright yellow stunt plane with red-and-orange flames painted on the side. It had over and under wings like a World War I biplane, the closed cockpit of a fighter jet, and a single prop in front.

"Now this is what I call *sweet*!" Jamal said.

"Are you talking about me or the plane?" asked a slender young woman stepping from the other side of the aircraft. She was dressed in a yellow-and-red aviator's jumpsuit, and had a pair of mirrored sunglasses pushed back on her head. Her straight black hair hung just above her shoulders, and her dark eyes twinkled. Her skin tone, hair, and eyes bespoke her Asian heritage.

"Both," Jamal said, recovering from minor shock. "I'm Jamal Hawkins, of Hawkins Air. These are my friends, Frank and Joe Hardy." He extended his hand, and she shook it.

"Nice to meet you," the woman said. "I'm Amy Chow." She patted the yellow airplane. "So you like the *Screamin' Demon*, eh?"

"It's a fine-looking plane," said Joe.

"Are you *the* Amy Chow?" Frank asked. "The big dot-com innovator?"

"*Former* dot-com innovator," Amy corrected him, smiling. "Now I'm Amy Chow, the cashed-out airplane-collecting multimillionaire. It's a tough job, but someone's got to do it."

"If you need someone to take over for you . . ." Jamal said.

She laughed. "The line forms to the rear."

"So, are you here collecting or showing off?" Joe asked.

"A bit of both," she replied, "same as everyone here. Yourselves?"

"Looking around," Frank answered, "and picking up a plane for Jamal's dad; he owns Hawkins Air Service."

"We're adding a Sullivan Brothers Air Customizing job to our line," Jamal added.

Amy whistled appreciatively. "Sweet fly. I've got one already, so I'm not in the market right now. I hear there'll be plenty of Sullivan customs at the show, though."

"One will be plenty for us," Joe replied slyly.

"One's never enough!" Amy said. "Well, gotta run. I see Clevon Brooks ambling this way, and he looks like he's in a bad mood. Catch you boys later. Oh, hey, don't get fingerprints on my plane." She smiled and started to head across the tarmac toward the administration building.

As she left, a tall, thin African-American man in a T-shirt, jeans, and a leather aviator's jacket covered with endorsement patches jogged up. "Have you seen Amy Chow around here?" he asked. "I need to talk to her."

"She just left," Frank said.

"Mr. Brooks," Jamal said, extending his hand, "I'm Jamal Hawkins from Hawkins Air. I admire your work very much."

Brooks shook his hand tentatively but kept looking around for Amy. "Thanks."

"That rear-prop swept-wing experimental plane you built was something!" Jamal enthused.

"Hey, thanks," Brooks said. "Look, I'd love to chat, but I really need to catch Ms. Chow." He jogged off toward the administration building.

"Is he often rude?" Joe asked when he'd gone.

"He's just eccentric," Jamal said, "but brilliant."

11

"I caught his work on an episode of *Nova* once," Frank said.

"I remember that," Joe replied. "He's big in the experimental aviation field."

"I wonder what kind of plane he's brought with him to the show," Jamal said. Then, spotting something, he added, "Hey, there's one of the Sullivan jobs over there."

The brothers looked toward a largish low-bellied single-prop plane with a top-mounted wing. Blue-and-gold piping decorated its sleek body.

"C'mon," Jamal said, "let's see if it's the one we're picking up."

"You don't know what color your plane is?" Joe asked.

Jamal shook his head. "Dad didn't mention it. I guess he was busy getting ready for his trip to China. The color doesn't matter, really. We're gonna paint it anyway. C'mon!"

He jogged off toward the blue-and-gold plane with the brothers following close behind.

Just then a brightly colored car screeched across the tarmac. It was heading straight for them.

2 Air Apparent

"Look out!" Frank shouted as the red-and-white Chevy barreled toward them.

Sunlight glinted off the car's shining chrome details. The Chevy's whitewall tires squealed on the airport's patchy tarmac.

The Hardys and Jamal dived aside as the car screeched to a halt, barely a few feet from where they'd been standing.

A stocky man with graying hair, wearing a white cowboy suit and hat and a blue shirt, got out of the driver's side of the car and laughed. "What's the matter?" he asked. "Did I frighten y'all?"

"Jack Meeker!" Jamal said angrily. "You are one first-class jerk!" He and the Hardys got up off the pavement and dusted themselves off.

"Nice seeing you too, young Hawkins," Jack Meeker replied. "Hey, I heard your pappy ducked out on this swap meet. Afraid of a little competition?"

"Not from *you*," Jamal shot back. "Dad's taking care of some business that you can't even *dream* about."

"That Asian charter tie-in?" Meeker said. "That hound don't hunt, son! I turned it down last week. Your pappy will be lucky if they don't sell him back the snake oil that they stole from him in the first place."

Jamal clenched his fists but said nothing.

"Ben Hawkins is an honest businessman," Frank said firmly.

"Maybe you should just mind your own business, whoever you are," Joe added.

Meeker looked mildly shocked. "Ain't you boys heard of me? You been livin' in a *barn*? I'm the king of local air taxis. Hawkins Air has been eatin' my dust for years."

"In your dreams, Meeker," Jamal said.

"Why do you think your pappy's buying that new airplane and gallivanting all around the world?" Meeker said. "He's trying to keep up with me, of course. Not doin' too good a job of it, though."

"You don't have to put up with this, Jamal," Joe said, balling up his fists.

Both Jamal and Joe seemed about to go after Meeker, but Frank stepped between them. "Take it easy, guys," he said. Then he said to Meeker, "Maybe you should leave."

Meeker smiled broadly. "Now don't get all riled up, boys," he said. "I don't mean no harm. I just came by to wish you a fine show. Good luck with that bucket of bolts I hear you're picking up for your pappy."

"Thanks," Jamal said, clearly not meaning it.

"Why don't you climb back into your own bucket of bolts and haul yourself out of here?" Joe added, indicating Meeker's classic car.

"I don't mind if I do," Meeker said. "I'm feeling a bit parched, if you git my drift. I'd invite you boys to join me, but I know you're underage." He hopped back into his car and roared away, blaring his horn as he went.

"I didn't know they made a car horn that played 'The Yellow Jerk of Texas,'" Frank said.

Jamal clenched his teeth. "That guy really burns me up."

"Anytime Meeker's clock needs cleaning," Joe said, "you just call me."

"So," Frank said, changing the subject, "is this the airplane your dad bought?"

Jamal gave the big blue-and-gold plane a good look, then shook his head. "Nah," he said. "The serial numbers are wrong. Wrong set of doors too. This one looks like someone's been modifying it from the original Sullivan customizing."

"Customizing a custom airplane," Joe said. "What'll they think of next?"

"Well, *I'm* thinking that we should check in at the campground," Frank said. "We can poke around the airfield and find the plane later. It might not even be here yet."

Jamal nodded. "Getting to the campground soon is probably a good idea."

"We wouldn't want them giving our tiny patch of bare ground to someone else," Joe said.

"It's getting pretty late in the afternoon too," Jamal said. "We need to get ready for the big welcome dinner. You guys bring your tuxes?" He flashed a smile.

All three of them laughed.

"Come on," Frank said. "Let's get checked in." They headed for the old motel.

It took a surprisingly long time to get checked in. The teenager working behind the desk wasn't very organized, and he'd misplaced their reservation information. The computer was down, and he had to check the records by hand.

By the time the three friends got their tent set up and their gear stowed away, it was nearly dark. They used their cell phones to call their parents and confirm their arrival at the show, then hiked back across the pitted tarmac toward the buildings at the far end of the airfield.

"They're holding the banquet in one of the

16

hangars near the control tower," Jamal said.

"Let's hope they cleaned the place first," Joe said, gazing at the ancient Quonset-style metal buildings. "This whole airport looks like it needs a year's worth of industrial-strength service from Mighty Maid."

"The cleaning service that 'Sweeps away your troubles and leaves you smiling,'" Frank said, quoting an old TV ad campaign.

The three friends passed by a number of interesting planes on their way to the opening banquet. None of them was the plane that Jamal was looking for, though. As they neared the banquet hall hangar, he spotted another plane at the far end of the field.

"Hey, maybe that's it," he said, pointing.

"The maroon-and-magenta job?" Joe replied. "I can't say I think much of the color scheme."

"We can check it out later," Frank said. "Unless you want to be fashionably late to this dinner."

"And miss the first course?" Jamal said. "Never!"

They entered the hangar through a double door near the front. The big open space inside had in fact been nicely cleaned up. The metal walls still looked a bit dingy, but the concrete floor practically shone. Star-spangled bunting and big banners with pictures of historic aircraft hung from the rafters. The brothers quickly spotted the Wright brothers' plane, Lindburgh's *Spirit of St. Louis,* and Chuck Yeager's rocket plane, which was the first to break the sound barrier.

The hangar floor held several rows of long tables. They all faced a small speaker's platform at one end of the building. Behind the podium rested a fully restored World War II Spitfire. The vintage plane looming in the background lent a nice atmosphere to the proceedings.

More than three hundred people were already in the room. They didn't fill the immense space but clustered around the tables in the center. The aviators gathered in small, tightly packed clumps, exchanging tips. Dinner had not yet begun, but the places had been set.

Amy Chow and Clevon Brooks were talking on one side of the room, near the big hangar door. Jack Meeker had Elise Flaubert cornered by the podium. The airport administrator smiled politely as they spoke, but her eyes seemed to be looking for an exit.

The Hardys and Jamal checked their table assignment and discovered, somewhat to their relief, that they were near the back of the assembly.

"If things get slow," Jamal whispered to his friends, "we can duck out early."

"Good plan," Joe said, nodding.

As they edged their way through the crowd toward their places, someone bumped into Frank, nearly knocking the elder Hardy over.

"Hey! Watch it!" barked a burly man in a battered flying jacket with a fleece collar.

"Why don't *you* watch where *you're* going?" Joe countered.

"No harm done," Frank said, stepping between the man and Joe.

"Hey, aren't you Dale 'Rock' Grissom?" Jamal said to the surly flier.

"Yeah. So?" the gruff man replied.

"I saw you do some stunt flying at a show when I was a kid," Jamal said. "You had some great reflexes."

"Still do, kid," Grissom replied. "Still do. Now, if you'll excuse me, I gotta see a man about some work." He continued pushing through the crowd.

"Not much for fans, is he?" Joe said, scowling.

Jamal shrugged. "Another hero with feet of clay, I guess. He was *something* when I first saw him, fresh out of the air force's secret test programs. Lightning response time."

The teens moved past a few intervening groups and found their place settings. As they arrived, a balding man sporting a goatee and wearing a blue jumpsuit intercepted them.

"Are you Jamal Hawkins?" he asked.

"That's me."

"Thought so," the man said, shaking hands with Jamal. "You look a lot like your dad. I'm Steve Davidson. I'm supposed to deliver a plane to you."

"Yeah," Jamal said, his face lighting up. "Where is it?"

"Outside," Davidson said. "It's that maroon-and-magenta baby near the end of the line."

"We spotted it coming in," Joe said.

Davidson pulled out a stack of papers and laid them on the table. "I need you to sign for the plane," he said, picking up one of the sheets and placing it in front of Jamal. He handed Jamal a pen. "Sorry for the rush. I've been trying to track you down for a couple of hours."

"We couldn't have been that hard to find," Frank said.

"To tell you the truth, kid," Davidson said, lowering his voice, "this show isn't very organized. If I hadn't found you now, I was gonna come back tomorrow. The office of my service is just down in Jewel Ridge."

"The plane's not yours?" Joe asked.

Davidson shook his head. "Nah. I'm just a middleman, mostly as a favor to Ben Hawkins. How's his China trip going, by the way?"

"Pretty well, I guess," Jamal replied. "He'll be back next week."

"Too bad I can't hang around until then," Davidson said. "In fact I can't even stick around for dinner. My ride's waiting outside. So, if you'll just sign here and take the keys . . ."

"We should check out the plane first," Frank said.

"Don't worry, guys," Jamal said. "Davidson's an old friend of Dad's. If he says it's okay, I'm sure it is."

"The Hawkins family knows where I live," Davidson said, smiling. "I wouldn't even *try* to put one over on them. I had the airport mechanic check the plane earlier, just in case. He says it's ready to fly."

"Great," Jamal said. He signed the delivery receipt and gathered up the keys and ownership papers. Davidson handed him a pouch to put the paperwork in. As he did, a waiter appeared on the other side of the table and laid down some bowls of pastry-topped French onion soup.

"Too bad I have to miss the chow," Davidson said. "Good luck with the plane, kid. You've got my office number if you need me. You'll find everything in order, though. She's a beaut."

"Aside from the paint job," Joe said.

Davidson laughed. "Yeah, aside from that." He shook hands with them and headed out the door.

"Smooth talker, that guy," Frank said.

"Yeah. He went to college with Dad. You should hear some of the stories about him." Jamal arched his eyebrows.

"Maybe after dinner," Joe said.

The teens took their seats and started the first course. Soon they were joined at their table by Clevon Brooks on one side and a businessman named Tony Manetti with his personal assistant, Rita Davenport, on the other. Manetti was a tall, solid-looking man with slicked-back hair. He wore a dark suit with thin pinstriping. Davenport was a pretty woman, with an attractive face and dishwater blond hair. Rose-tinted glasses, which almost matched the color of her dress suit, partially obscured her gray eyes.

"You guys seem pretty young to be attending the show," Ms. Davenport said after they'd finished their salads. "Are you shopping or showing?"

"We're picking up a Sullivan custom plane," Jamal said.

"Oh, yeah?" Mr. Manetti replied. "You're not another dot-com millionaire, like that Chow girl, are you?"

The Hardys and Jamal laughed. "No," Frank said, "we're just helping out Jamal's dad."

"Good," Manetti said, relieved. "I'm getting sick of meeting kids who're richer than me! That Sullivan job you're picking up—is it a good plane?"

"One of the best," Jamal replied.

"Mr. Manetti's shopping for smaller planes at this show," Ms. Davenport said, "but maybe we'll check out a Sullivan sometime."

"This would be a good place for it," Joe said. "We've seen quite a few at the show already."

The rest of the dinner was excellent, though the conversation flagged during the main course, stuffed pork chops. As dessert arrived, the presentation began. Opening remarks by Elise Flaubert gave way to a lecture on the future of aviation by

Dr. Sirkin, a former space shuttle mission specialist and professor from Cal Tech.

Brooks abruptly excused himself during the speech. "Old rival," Rita Davenport whispered to the teens. She and Manetti didn't stay much longer, though. "Long day tomorrow," Manetti explained.

The professor gave a good speech, and Jamal and the brothers sat in rapt attention. After Dr. Sirkin finished, though, the talks quickly became less interesting and more technical. The Hardys noticed Jamal's eyes straying toward the exit.

"Let's head out," Frank whispered, "and check out Jamal's new plane."

"Sounds good to me," Jamal replied.

Joe nodded his agreement, and the three boys quietly left the big hangar. The air outside was nippy, and their breath hovered like ghosts over their heads.

"Maybe we should stay in the plane rather than on the campground," Jamal said, zipping up his old fleece-collared aviator jacket.

"Where's your sense of adventure?" Joe kidded him.

"Frozen, I think," Jamal replied.

"That new Sullivan custom will get your heart beating again, I bet," Frank said. He jogged across the airfield toward where they'd seen the maroon-and-magenta plane parked. Joe and Jamal followed.

As they passed by the brick administration office, though, Joe suddenly stopped.

"What is it?" Frank asked.

"I just saw a flashlight beam across those frosted windows," Joe said.

"You think there's a power outage?" Jamal asked.

Frank shook his head. "The exit light's working. Power's working. So I'm thinking someone's sneaking around."

3 Unscheduled Appointment

"Check the front door," Frank said. They moved quickly to the main entrance of the administration building.

"Locked," Jamal said, trying the door.

"It could be a security guard," Joe remarked.

"We won't know unless we check it out," Frank said. "Let's try the back."

"I'll stick around here," Jamal said, "in case whoever it is comes out."

"Good plan," said Joe. "Stay alert."

"Shivering will keep me awake."

Frank smiled. "I'm betting your aviator jacket is warmer than our letterman jackets."

"I'll take that bet after you catch this guy," Jamal said. "Now get going before I freeze to death!"

The brothers quickly hiked around the side of the building to the rear entrance. The window where Joe had seen the light was on the second floor, which occupied only the rear corner of the building. A flat roof near the front doubled as an observation deck, with a patio table, chairs, and—incongruously, considering the time of year—a big lounge umbrella in the middle.

The Hardys passed beneath the window as they went, but they saw no more lights. They quietly tried the lock on the rear door.

"Taped open," Frank whispered.

The brothers crept into the darkened building and quickly found an exit stairway leading up. After cautiously mounting the steps, they entered a short corridor running between two pairs of second-floor offices. The offices had frosted glass windows and doors. ELISE FLAUBERT—ADMINISTRATOR was painted on the glass of one door. A slender beam of light peeked out from under that door.

Frank and Joe each stood on either side of the door, and Frank put his hand on the doorknob. On a silent count of three, he pushed the door open, and both brothers barged into the darkened office.

"Hold it!" Frank said, speaking to a figure lurking in the dark shadows on the far side of the room.

"What's going on here?" Joe asked, trying to make out the identity of the black shape behind the desk.

Instead of answering, the intruder doused his

flashlight and dashed his hand across the desk. Papers filled the air. The plastic in-out box sailed past the Hardys and smashed against the far wall. As the brothers ducked to avoid the impromptu missile, the burglar opened a sliding door behind the desk and ran out onto the rooftop terrace.

Skidding on the spilled papers, the brothers scrambled across the room and out the door after him. The burglar ran across the roof, grabbed on to the ledge, and lowered himself onto the side of the building.

"Jamal!" Joe called. "Cut him off!"

"Cut who—ow!" Jamal's startled voice drifted up from below.

The brothers reached the side of the building and lowered themselves just as Jamal got to his feet again. "I didn't see him coming," he explained. "He knocked me down. Took the wind right out of me."

"Who was it?" Joe asked.

"I didn't get a good look," Jamal replied. "He was dressed in black and was wearing a ski mask." He leaned against the side of the building and tried to catch his breath.

"Call security!" Frank shouted back to him. Both Hardys took off after the rapidly disappearing figure.

The burglar moved quickly. He darted between two of the planes lined up along the edge of the tarmac and went into one of the dark hangars.

The Hardys opened the hangar door, then jumped

back as a falling metal bucket clanged onto the floor.

"Nice makeshift trap," Joe said, eyeing the big metal pail on the floor.

"You can compliment him *after* we catch him," Frank replied.

Careful of more traps, they moved quickly into the interior of the hangar.

"Shoot! I can't see anything in here," Joe said.

"I think I hear him toward the back," Frank said, heading in that direction.

The old metal hangar housed a number of planes, their hulking shapes obscuring the room beyond. Large, rectangular shapes loomed out of the darkness—toolboxes, the brothers assumed from their silhouettes. Air and water hoses and power cords snaked across the floor. The Hardys had to move cautiously so as not to trip.

"There's a door in the back," Joe said.

"I see the exit light," Frank replied, "but I don't see anyone."

"He couldn't have gotten out any other way," Joe said. He moved to the door while Frank kept watch behind them.

"It's unlocked," Joe said, "and I hear someone outside."

He and Frank burst through the door into the alley behind. As they exited, they nearly plowed into a swarthy man with a dark bandanna, who was pushing a trash cart and toting a broom. Lettering above the pocket on the man's jumpsuit read "Jose." The man looked startled to see the teens, but didn't appear to be in any hurry to leave.

"Did you see someone come this way?" Joe asked.

Jose shook his head. "No," he replied. "No one has come this way."

Frank's eyes narrowed. "Are you sure? What are you doing here?"

"I'm doing my job," Jose said. "I clean the hangars at night. What are *you* doing here?"

"We were chasing someone who broke into the administration building," Joe said.

Jose's eyes widened. "That's very bad," he said. "You have contacted security, yes?"

"We sent for them," Frank replied. "Are you sure you didn't see anyone?"

"I am sure."

The brothers looked around but saw no sign of anyone else behind the hangar. There were several smaller maintenance buildings nearby, but no trace of the intruder.

Frank scratched his head. "We've lost him," the elder Hardy said. He and Joe took a final look through the deserted hangar, then headed back toward the administration building.

"I'd have suspected that janitor," Joe said as they walked, "but he wasn't sweating or breathing hard."

"There must have been some other way out of the hangar that we didn't spot," Frank said.

They saw a light on in the administrator's office when they arrived. Having gone up the back stairs once again, they found Elise Flaubert and Jamal standing in the center of the office, amid the scattered papers. With them was a middle-aged, droopy-faced security guard whose badge read "Mitchum."

"So, you didn't get a good look at who did this?" Mitchum asked Jamal.

"Sorry," Jamal replied. "He knocked me down before I could recognize him. My friends, Frank and Joe, went after him, though."

"But we didn't catch him," Frank said, entering the room.

"Sorry," Joe added. "He lost us in one of the hangars."

"Well," Ms. Flaubert said, "it doesn't look as if anything's been taken. These show registration papers are in a real mess, though."

"Why would someone break in, then not take anything?" Frank asked.

"I'll ask the questions here," Mitchum said. "You think you're a detective or something? Maybe you boys interrupted this thief before he could take anything."

"Why mess up the place then?" Joe asked.

"Maybe he couldn't find what he was looking for," Mitchum replied. "Is the safe okay, Elise?"

Elise Flaubert opened a closet in one wall to

reveal a bulky old safe about the size of a minifridge. "Looks fine," she said.

"The cops will want to talk to you boys," Mitchum said, noticing the flashing red-and-blue lights appearing outside the frosted windows. "You all wait here. I'm going to check the grounds and see if I can find any clues."

"Good luck," Frank said.

Mitchum scowled at him.

"Has the welcoming dinner finished?" Joe asked Ms. Flaubert.

"No," she replied. "I had stepped out to attend to some business when I ran into Jamal. I hope this doesn't turn into a big incident; I don't want anything to disrupt the show."

"I think that's probably up to the police," Frank said, looking at the stern-faced officer coming through the office door.

It took the three friends about an hour to run through with the police all that had happened. The banquet was finally wrapping up by then, but Elise Flaubert managed to keep the break-in from becoming the talk of the show. By the time Jamal and the brothers finally made it to the new Hawkins Air plane, most of the air-show goers had left Scott Field for the night.

"The paint looks almost *black* now," Jamal noted as they approached the plane.

"A distinct improvement," Joe commented.

"Many shades of red look black in dim light," Frank said. "Human color perception is distorted in the darkness."

"Joe's right," Jamal said. "It's an improvement. When we get home, the first thing I'm doing is arranging to have it painted."

The maroon-and-magenta Sullivan aircraft may have been ugly on the outside, but inside, it was a dream. The teens entered through the passenger door in the rear and worked their way toward the front. The eight passenger seats in the former Cessna Caravan were fine Spanish leather. The side paneling was highly polished wood, with exquisite inlaid geometric details. A wet bar and minifridge had been built into one wall. The area between the cabin and the cockpit featured a state-of-the-art entertainment center.

Joe whistled appreciatively. "Your dad must have paid a pretty penny for this," he said to Jamal.

"I ask him no questions, and he doesn't raid my college account," Jamal said, smiling.

Wooden detailing dominated the control panels, and the pilot and copilot seats were just as lush and comfortable as the passenger seats.

"This is the only way to fly," Frank said.

"If you play your cards right," Jamal said, "I might take you for a spin."

"Forget *taking* us," Joe said. "I want to fly this baby myself."

"That, I'm afraid, is something my dad would *kill* me for doing," Jamal said.

"A guy can dream, can't he?" Joe sighed.

They admired the plane for the better part of an hour, enjoying the plush appointments and checking out the controls. Then, after satisfying themselves that Davidson had been as good as his word, they made their way back to the tiny campground at the north edge of the airfield.

Only a few other tents stood pitched in the small yard beside the Flyboy Motel, and several motor homes were parked just off the motel's gravel driveway. Most of the other show attendees, it seemed, preferred warmer accommodations.

"Man, I should just sleep in the Sullivan tonight," Jamal said, his teeth chattering.

"If you want to, go for it," Joe replied.

Jamal shook his head. "No way I'm going to have you guys saying I wussed out because of a little cold weather. Warm the tent up a bit with the heater, and I'll be fine."

Frank and Joe did as Jamal asked. In a few minutes the tent was toasty warm. They turned off the heater, huddled into their sleeping bags, and the three of them quickly fell asleep.

Around two in the morning they were awakened by a loud thrumming, buzzing noise.

"What's that?" Joe asked.

"Sounds like a plane on the runway," Jamal said. "Who'd be taking off at this time of the night?"

"That's not just *any* plane on the runway," Frank said, who had poked his head through the tent flaps and was peering outside. "It's *your* plane!"

4 One of Our Planes Is Missing

Joe and Jamal pulled back the tent flaps and gazed out to see what Frank was looking at.

Sure enough, a big Sullivan custom plane was taxiing down the tarmac toward the runway. Only the faint lights leaking from surrounding buildings lit the runway. The ugly maroon-and-magenta paint still looked black in the dim light, but there was no mistaking the plane.

"Come on!" Frank said, bolting out into the night. Joe and Jamal followed right behind him, quickly accelerating into a sprint. The three teenagers were trained athletes with impressive speed, and the gap between them and the plane closed quickly.

Fortunately the boys had worn their clothes to

bed to fend off the autumn chill. Unfortunately they hadn't worn shoes, and the cold pavement felt like ice beneath their socks.

The stolen plane reached one end of the runway just as the boys reached the other. The Hardys and Jamal dashed down the worn concrete toward the oncoming plane. The plane accelerated, its engine roared, and its central prop spun into a nearly invisible blur.

While Jamal stood in shock, Frank and Joe waved their arms and shouted to get the pilot to stop the plane. It merely picked up speed. The darkness made it impossible to see who was behind the controls.

"They're not slowing down!" Joe said.

"Look out!" Frank cried.

The three boys leaped out of the way just in time. The Sullivan custom barreled past them toward the far end of the runway.

The friends picked themselves up off the tarmac and ran after the plane, but it was no use. The stolen aircraft lifted smoothly into the chilly fall air. The three teens stood on the pavement, unable to do anything but watch.

"I was wrong earlier," Jamal said forlornly. "My dad's going to kill me for *this*."

"You're not dead yet," Frank replied. "We might still catch them, using your old plane."

"I'll grab the keys," Jamal said. "You guys prep it

for takeoff." While he dashed back toward the tent, the Hardys ran for the Cessna 182 that they'd arrived in.

Frank and Joe pulled the chock blocks out from under the wheels and did a quick preflight inspection of the exterior.

"Hey, you!" a gruff voice called. "Get away from that plane!"

The brothers spun and saw Mitchum, the security guard, loping toward them out of the darkness. His face was red from exertion and slightly puffy, as though he'd just woken up.

"But this is our friend's plane," Joe said.

"So *you* say," Mitchum replied. "You also claimed to have seen a burglar in the administration office earlier. What's your connection with the plane that just took off?"

"That's our friend's plane too," Frank said.

"Oh," Mitchum replied, arching his bushy eyebrows skeptically. "*That's* your friend's plane, *this* is your friend's plane. . . . Is there any plane on this airfield that your 'friend' doesn't own?"

"We're telling the truth," Joe said, frustration building in his voice.

"Take it easy, kid," Mitchum said, his fingers resting on the butt of his gun.

"Look," Frank said, "both this plane and the stolen one are owned by Hawkins Air Service. Our friend, Jamal Hawkins, had to get his keys so we can chase the plane that was just stolen. Look, here he comes now."

Jamal dashed up to the group. He had the keys to the plane in his hand, but he still didn't have any shoes on. "C'mon," he said, "let's get going!"

"You kids aren't going anywhere," Mitchum said. "Not until I figure out what's going on here."

"By then it'll be too late!" Joe said.

Mitchum eyed Jamal from the top of his head to his socks. "You don't look old enough to own *any* planes, kid," the guard said. "Amy Chow is at least four years older than you, and she's the youngest owner at this fly-in."

Jamal bounced impatiently on the balls of his feet. "They're my dad's planes. We need to use this one to catch the other one."

"I think I better call Ms. Flaubert about this," Mitchum said, pulling out a combination cell phone walkie-talkie with one hand, and keeping the other hand on the butt of his gun.

"There's no time!" Jamal protested.

"Kid," Mitchum said with a weary smile, "there's *always* time."

Jamal was right. By the time they got the situation straightened out with Mitchum and Ms. Flaubert, the stolen plane was long gone. Flaubert called the police, and the friends repeated the story of what happened. The cops seemed almost as skeptical as Mitchum had been.

The police went through the motions, filled out paperwork and contacted the proper authorities, but no one seemed to believe that the stolen plane would be found quickly.

"It was heading north by northwest when it dropped off the radar," Ms. Flaubert said, "but that was so soon after takeoff that it could be almost anywhere now."

"If only we could have gotten into the air and chased it," Joe said, clearly frustrated.

"Sorry, kid," Mitchum said. "Next time put on your shoes before you go running around like crazy people. That way at least you'll look a bit more credible."

Frank put his hand on Jamal's shoulder. "Don't worry. We'll find that plane, and whoever took it, before your dad gets back from China."

"I sure hope so," Jamal said. "I *knew* I should have slept in that plane tonight."

"We'll alert the fliers coming in and out of the show to keep their eyes peeled for it," Flaubert said. "The police will have people out looking as well. If there's anything else we can do, don't hesitate to ask."

"Would you call my dad for me and explain all this?" Jamal asked jokingly.

Jamal had trouble reaching his dad and decided not to leave a message with his service. "What am I going to say?" he asked. "'Sorry, Dad, but your new plane got stolen, and the cops have no leads. Call me back when you get a chance.' I hope he paid the insurance before he left!"

"I'm sure he did," Frank said.

"Your father's a very reliable guy," Joe told his friend. "Just like his son."

"I don't feel so reliable at the moment," Jamal replied.

"Some sleep will do you a world of good," Frank said. "We'll tackle finding the stolen plane in the morning."

They went back to the campground and crawled into their sleeping bags, but none of the boys slept much during the remainder of the night.

They rose with the sun. It was still cold outside; the red rays of dawn didn't chase the chill away from the frigid autumn morning.

Jamal and the brothers dressed warmly, then checked on the Cessna 182. They saw an occasional patrol car circling the field and noticed another security guard patrolling along with a very tired-looking Mitchum.

"Too little too late," Jamal noted bitterly.

"Don't give up," Frank said. "Let's take the plane and search. Maybe we can spot something."

Jamal nodded. "I'll fuel up on the company credit card," he said.

"I don't think the Scott Field fuel wagon is out

yet," Joe said. "Do you have enough in the tank?"

"Plenty, so long as we don't fly into another state," Jamal replied. "We can fill up when we get back."

The three of them piled into the airplane. A controller cleared them for takeoff, and they launched into the air. Jamal set their course along the same heading as the stolen plane, using the coordinates Ms. Flaubert had estimated the previous evening.

The hills to the north of Scott Field became steeper and progressively more wooded. Patches of snow on the ground became more frequent, and the ponds below them took on a glittering sheen of new ice.

"Hey, Joe," Jamal called back to the rear of the Cessna, "what's up ahead?" Frank was flying copilot that morning.

Joe, sitting in one of the rear seats, checked their map. "Lots of woods and hills," he replied. "Kendall State Park . . . and beyond that, the Berkshires."

"Nice place to visit," Jamal said.

"Bad place to look for a plane, though," Frank commented. "A stolen aircraft would be easy to conceal in those woods."

"The trick would be landing it in one piece," Jamal said. "Hey, there's an old airstrip by that farm down there."

The brothers looked out the window and spotted a tiny runway with a rusty fuel tank next to it.

Nearby stood a battered farmhouse and several overgrown fields.

"Looks deserted," Joe said. "No sign of the plane either."

"And there's no way they could hide a plane in that," Frank said, indicating a pile of boards and rubble that had once been a barn.

"Maybe they swung south, and the northwest course was just a decoy," Jamal said. He turned the plane around, and they circled back around Scott Field from the other end.

A short while later they still hadn't found any sign of the missing plane. Frustrated, they returned to the Fly By & Buy air show.

"I'll fuel up so we can go out again later on," Jamal said after they'd landed.

"We'll grab some grub," Joe said, "and meet you back here."

Jamal nodded, and they all went about their errands.

The early morning sun had risen higher during the friends' brief flight, but most of the air show attendees were still waking up. The smell of coffee permeated the air, and rumpled-looking aviators mumbled greetings as they passed each other on the tarmac.

The airport cafeteria was an old cinder block building behind the row of big metal hangars. It wasn't too far from where the Hardys had chased the office intruder the night before. Frank and Joe walked between two of the hangars toward the alleyway between the buildings.

As they neared the alley, angry voices drifted through the chilly autumn air.

"That sounds like Clevon Brooks," Frank said.

"And Rock Grissom," added Joe. "What are they saying?"

"Hang back. Let's find out," Frank whispered.

They moved cautiously to the edge of the hangar and peeked around the corner.

Grissom and Brooks stood nearly nose to nose in the alleyway between the hangars and the service buildings. Both men looked angry.

As the brothers watched, Grissom seized Brooks by the collar and aimed a fist at the aviation innovator's face.

5 Ace Cadet vs. Space Cadet

Joe took a step forward as if to break up the fight, but Frank held him back. "Hang on," he whispered.

As Frank spoke, Brooks shook himself free from Grissom's grasp and backed up. Joe retreated behind the hangar.

"You've gone too far this time, Dale," Brooks said, pointing his finger at the leather-clad jet jockey. "Just back off!"

"You're lucky I don't clean your intakes, Brooks," Grissom replied.

"You promised you'd hire me to test your new experimental planes. I was counting on that contract. I *need* that contract!"

"I know this may come as news to you, Dale," Brooks said, "but I have needs too. One of the things

I need is for my company not to go broke. I've struggled over the years, and I'll make it through this setback too. Perhaps when things turn around, I'll still hire you—if you can control your temper."

"Whether I control my temper depends a lot on what you have to say," Grissom replied.

"My situation has changed," Brooks said. "I can't afford to hire you now. If I did, I might very well sink the company."

"That ain't fair," Grissom said. "I was counting on that money."

"And I was counting on a number of circumstances that failed to materialize," Brooks said. "I sympathize with your situation, Dale. In fact I fear that I'm nearly in the same situation myself."

"Nearly," Grissom snarled. "Ha!"

Brooks straightened his endorsement-covered jacket. "If you're hard up for cash, perhaps you should consider selling your airplane," he said. "Sullivan customs are gaining popularity in the market right now. You could buy a smaller plane and still have plenty left to cover your bills."

"I'd rather run you into the ground than sell my plane," Grissom said.

"Fortunately, I won't give you that chance," Brooks said. He stepped back and held up his fists to fight.

Grissom lunged forward and tackled him.

The two aviators were rolling around on the

ground when the Hardys ran out from between the buildings. Joe grabbed Grissom, and Frank took hold of Brooks. The brothers pulled the two combatants away from each other.

"Back off!" Joe said.

"Get out of here!" said Grissom. "This is between that lying scum and me."

"Keep this up, and it'll be between you and the cops," Joe replied.

The younger Hardy's words brought both men to a halt. The two aviators stopped struggling, and the brothers let them go.

"This isn't over between us," Grissom said to Brooks.

"Have your lawyers look into it if you like," Brooks replied. "I've done nothing illegal. If you touch me again, though, I'll sue."

The two glared at each other before heading down the alley in opposite directions.

"Well," Joe said, watching them go, "we've had a break-in, a stolen plane, and now a fistfight. How do they all fit together?"

"Maybe they don't," Frank said. "Any show this big is bound to have some conflicting personalities. Let's round up some food and get back to Jamal."

They walked up the alley a short way and cut between two cinder block buildings to get to the airport commissary. The cafeteria was far too small to serve all the show attendees, so a big tent had been set up in front of it to deal with the overflow. A chow line inside the cinder block house doled out bacon and eggs, doughnuts, melon, and other traditional breakfast foods, along with cups of steaming coffee and hot chocolate.

The brothers picked up some bagels with cream cheese, a few oranges, and three cups of cocoa before heading back to the tarmac. They found Jamal polishing the body of the Hawkins Air plane with a damp chamois cloth. He smiled wanly when he saw the Hardys. "Not many bugs out this time of year," he said, "but at least it takes my mind off the missing plane." He stashed the chamois under the pilot's seat, and the Hardys broke out the breakfast. "That food smells great."

"We're on a tight budget," Frank said, "but at least it's enough to keep us sharp."

"Next time," Jamal said, "I'll ask my dad for a real expense account. Assuming he ever lets me do this again."

"Don't worry. We'll get you out of this jam," Joe replied.

As the three of them ate their breakfast in the Cessna's open cabin, Amy Chow sauntered over. "Hey, Hawkins," she said. "Was it your plane that got stolen last night?"

"I wish it were," Jamal replied.

Amy looked puzzled.

"It was his dad's plane," Frank explained.

"Oh," she said sympathetically, "that's much worse."

"Yeah," Jamal said. "We didn't even get a chance to take it for a spin before it got hijacked. Tell me that you dropped by to replace my plane for free."

"We could use a generous millionaire benefactor right about now," Joe remarked.

Amy laughed and shook her head. "Sorry, guys. No bailout from me today. I guess you'll just have to settle for being part of the Sullivan Brothers mystique."

"The Sullivan Brothers mystique?" Jamal echoed.

"What's that?" Joe asked.

"Planes customized by the Sullivan Brothers have a reputation in the industry. Sure, they're posh sky cruisers and all that. They're among the best planes available. But they've been owned by quite a number of crackpot flyboys—like Clevon Brooks, for instance."

"I didn't know Brooks had a Sullivan Brothers plane," Jamal said.

"Yeah, it's that fancy modified job with the big door on the side," Amy said.

"So is there more to this mystique," Frank asked, "or is it just that eccentrics prefer nice planes?"

Amy crinkled her nose at him. "Well, a robber named Dennis Carlson once used a Sullivan plane to escape from a police dragnet. He was employed by the Sullivan Brothers company, and he stole one right out of their hangar. The cops never caught him, and nobody ever saw that plane again."

"Except in aviator ghost stories, I suppose," Joe said, winking at Frank. "You're sure this isn't an urban legend?"

Amy shrugged. "A lot of myths grow up around the flying business. That's one of the things that make it so much fun. So, what do you guys have on your agenda today?"

"Well, we were hoping to catch a bit of the show . . ." Frank began.

"But now it looks like we'll be spending most of our time in the air looking for the stolen plane," Jamal finished.

"Bummer. Well, just steer clear of me while I'm performing," Chow said.

"You're flying in the show today?" Joe asked.

"Provided nobody steals my plane," Amy replied. "I'm not very impressed with the security around here."

"Me neither," said Frank. "It seems like they've only got one or two guys working the whole show."

"And Mitchum doesn't strike me as a really sharp whip," Joe added.

"I've heard," Amy said, "that the show is really strapped for cash. That's why they chose this out-of-the-way location for it. Heck, the main organizers aren't even *here*. They've delegated all their tasks to Elise Flaubert."

"She strikes me as pretty overwhelmed by the whole thing," Frank said.

"Wouldn't you be?" Amy asked. "You go from being the administrator of a struggling airstrip to doing that *plus* coordinating a major show. It's a tough job, and I'm glad I'm not doing it."

"So what are you doing in the show today?" Jamal asked.

"Aerobatics," she replied, a big grin breaking across her face. "You've seen my plane, the *Screamin' Demon.*"

"The fancy red-and-yellow biplane," Joe said.

"That's it. I'm going to take her up and put her through her paces. After that I intend to settle back and enjoy the rest of the show. Maybe do a bit of shopping."

Jamal arched one eyebrow. "For airplanes?"

She smiled. "What else? You boys could help me prep the *Demon* if you want."

"We'd love to . . ." Joe began.

"But we've got to look for our lost plane," Frank finished.

Amy smacked her forehead. "Right! You told me that. Good luck with your search, boys. Drop by and catch my show if you can."

"We'll try," Jamal replied.

Amy hurried off toward where they'd last seen the *Screamin' Demon* parked. The three friends finished their food, then checked over the Cessna, making sure it was ready to go up again. They paused only long enough to stretch their legs.

"There are more Sullivan planes here than I first thought," Frank said after returning from a brief walk.

"Almost enough to make a squadron," Joe added.

"I didn't think there were that many made," Jamal said. "Just my rotten luck the thieves picked mine to steal. We'll have to search pretty quickly. They're restricting the airspace above the field once today's air demos start."

They stowed some gear aboard, then took to the air. This time they covered the areas to the south and east. Unfortunately they had no more luck than they'd had that morning.

By the time they returned to Scott Field, the show fliers had begun to take to the air. The three friends sneaked in under the flight curfew and taxied to their spot alongside the runway. Before picking a good spot to watch the show, the three boys grabbed some lunch. They managed to avoid Jack Meeker at the commissary and steered clear of Clevon Brooks, who was arguing with a technician who had been manning the fuel truck.

Amy's *Screamin' Demon* took to the skies just as they settled in near their campsite at the old motel.

The red-and-yellow stunt plane climbed swiftly

into the air, doing a quick barrel roll as it cleared the tree line.

"Whoa," Jamal said. "My dad would kill me if I tried something like that."

The *Demon* climbed nearly straight up, practically stalled, then twisted and dipped right in a falling leaf maneuver. The biplane fluttered from side to side, descending a couple of thousand feet before Amy put it into a tight left turn.

She pulled out of the turn and into another barrel roll, then shot back toward the clouds once more. A quick Immelmann half loop turned the plane around, and Amy headed back toward Scott Field.

As she started another climb, however, the plane's engine stalled. The stunt plane nosed up, and its tail dipped back. It slipped to the side, flipped over, and plummeted straight toward the ground.

6 Down in Flames

"I don't think that's part of the show!" Jamal exclaimed.

"Ms. Chow's a good pilot," Frank said. "Maybe it's just a spectacular stunt."

"Not with the engine out," Jamal replied. "Look how she's fighting for control!"

As the three teens watched, the plane wobbled and wove in the air. The engine remained off, and the red-and-yellow stunt flier's nose headed straight for the ground.

Joe stood, his body tense. "There has to be something we can do!"

Frank shook his head. "She's got to pull out of this on her own—if she can."

Time stretched to a crawl as the plane plunged

toward the forested hills beyond the north runway. Slowly, ever so slowly, the nose of the *Screamin' Demon* began to inch up.

"She's doing it!" Jamal said.

"She's really close to the trees," Joe said.

The plane leveled out barely a hundred yards above the treetops. Amy angled it for the runway.

"She's coming in too fast," Frank said. "She's not going to make it!"

All eyes on the airfield focused on the plane as it fluttered, like an injured bird, toward the airstrip. At the last instant Amy pulled the nose up, and the landing gear touched down.

The plane hit hard. One of the wheel struts broke, and the *Demon* skidded along the runway, sending a spray of sparks into the air. It flashed past the old motel and campground and headed toward a row of planes lined up at the edge of the tarmac.

"Come on!" Joe said, sprinting after the plane. Frank and Jamal followed.

The plane spun in tight circles as it skidded in. The other wheel strut broke, and the belly of the aircraft smashed into the ground. The fuselage broke near the tail, and the plane bent in half like a jackknifed semitrailer.

Sparks filled the air, and flames sprang up near the broken tail section. The plane finally skidded to a stop about thirty yards from a row of show planes.

Rescue sirens filled the air as the Hardys and Jamal dashed toward the burning aircraft. The three boys were the first to arrive at the crash scene. The heat from the fire was uncomfortable. The pilot's cabin was intact, but there was no sign of movement inside.

"Give me a hand here!" Frank shouted, peering into the cockpit. The plane's automatic safety system had deployed upon impact, and cream-colored air bags shrouded the compartment. Inside, Amy Chow was groaning. Her helmeted head slumped to one side. "She's alive, but the catch is jammed." He tried to open the compartment but then pulled his hands away from the lever and shook them. "It's hot too!"

Joe took off his letterman jacket and wrapped it around his hands. Jamal did the same with his leather aviator coat. Jamal grabbed the lever and yanked it hard while Joe seized the edge of the stuck canopy and heaved.

The cockpit hatch flew open. Frank reached in and dragged Amy out of the burning plane. Joe and Jamal took her legs and helped Frank carry her away from the fiery aircraft.

"Bet when she painted the flames on the side of that bird, Amy didn't know it'd be prophetic," Jamal said as they laid her gently on the dry grass at the edge of the tarmac.

Amy groaned.

"The plane's safety systems probably saved her life," Joe said.

"Her piloting did too," Frank added. "I doubt I could have pulled out of a dive like that."

"Me neither," Jamal said. "I wonder what went wrong with the plane."

At that moment Amy's brown eyes flickered open. She glanced around feverishly and tried to stand up. "What happened?" she said. "Where's the *Demon*?"

"Totaled," Joe replied. "We pulled you out of the wreck."

"The engine quit, and I lost control," she said. "I couldn't steer the plane!"

"Take it easy," Frank said. "An ambulance is on the way."

Fire and rescue teams, which had been stationed at the field as a safety precaution during the show, arrived moments later. Firefighters began to hose down the remains of the *Screamin' Demon* as emergency medical technicians raced to Amy's side.

"Good work getting her out of that plane," the lead EMT said to Frank. "We'll take it from here."

The Hardys and Jamal backed away to give the medical personnel space to work.

"I'm okay," Amy kept saying. "I'm okay."

Elise Flaubert arrived shortly after the EMTs. The airport administrator eyed the group of medical technicians gathered around Amy but had the good sense not to interfere. "How is she?" Flaubert asked the brothers and Jamal. "Is she going to be okay?"

"I think so," Frank said.

"She didn't seem too badly hurt," Joe added. "But there might be internal injuries."

"What are you going to do to protect these other planes?" shouted a gruff voice. The teens and Flaubert turned and saw Jack Meeker striding across the tarmac toward them. Tony Manetti was following close behind. Neither man looked pleased.

"We need more fire trucks," Meeker said. "The fire could spread to the other planes near the runway."

"People have a lot of money tied up in those planes," Manetti added.

"The rest of the Scottsville Fire Department is already on the way," Flaubert said. "They've called for assistance from Jewel Ridge too. We're doing everything we can."

"What about the show?" asked Rock Grissom, striding up to the group. "Some of us need to make a living here."

Flaubert looked flustered. She glanced nervously around the field to where a handful of police and hired security agents were working to keep people away from the crash scene. "We'll do everything we can to keep the show going," she said. "The other runways aren't affected. We should be able to continue with the rest of the day's events."

"Is that wise?" Frank asked.

"Butt out, kid," Grissom said. "You ain't got a stake in this show, like the rest of us."

"We'll continue if at all possible," Flaubert said. "Now if you'll excuse me, I need to coordinate with the emergency services." She turned on her heel and walked back toward the hangars near the administration building. Manetti, Grissom, and Meeker trailed after her, still badgering her and asking questions. Meeker shot a parting sneer at Jamal and the Hardys.

"Nice to see everyone is keeping this in perspective," Joe said, meaning just the opposite. He, Frank, and Jamal looked toward the chaos on the far side of the field. Attendees and spectators mingled with newly arrived police and fire units.

"I'll be amazed if this isn't the end of the show for the day," Frank said.

"I dunno," Joe said. "Never underestimate the power of ambitious people." He and the others watched as the ambulance carrying Amy left the field.

"Come on," said Jamal. "We'd better check the Cessna. It'd be just my luck to have one plane stolen and another smashed up by debris or antsy crowds on the same day."

The boys skirted around the police and fire lines and pushed their way through the milling crowds to the old Hawkins Air Service plane. They were pleased to discover it in one piece.

The same could not be said, however, for all the planes in the area. They overheard several people complaining to the police that their planes had been broken into during the commotion.

The three friends stayed with the Cessna until the crowds thinned out. By midafternoon the blaze consuming the *Screamin' Demon* had been extinguished, and the wreckage of the plane had been carted away. Grounds crews were still working on the north runway, but the other runways were open for business.

Two hours later Elise Flaubert, looking haggard but sporting a smile, announced that the Fly By & Buy would continue with its late-afternoon and evening schedule of events. An investigator from the National Transportation Safety Board (NTSB) arrived to look into the crash. He gave some orders and went over the scene briefly before cordoning the area off and going to the hospital to speak with Amy Chow.

The news about Amy was encouraging. Reports on the radio confirmed that—miraculously—she hadn't been seriously injured in the crash. The buzz around the airport was that she was intending to return to the show as soon as she could.

"Well, I guess if you need to shop for a new plane," Joe noted, "this is the place to do it."

Despite the good news about Amy, the mood at Scott Field remained grim. A number of planes had been damaged by debris from the crash, and the simultaneous break-ins away from the disaster had many show attendees on edge.

"A lot of pricey custom planes were hit," the teens overheard Rock Grissom say. "You can bet I'll be keeping both eyes on my aircraft from now on."

"I wouldn't make too much of this," Tony Manetti replied. "Most of the custom jobs happened to be parked on that side of the field. A thief would have had to take whatever was available."

The two men walked away, continuing their conversation in hushed tones.

"Think there's anything to that?" Jamal asked.

"It could be like Manetti said," Joe replied.

"And it would make sense for thieves to hit the most expensive planes," said Frank.

"Which leaves our old Cessna out," Jamal said. "I suppose I should be glad for small favors."

The Hardys and Jamal took a short break at the campground. Their full schedule during the day so far had left them pretty beat. As the afternoon edged toward evening, they headed back to the show.

"I want to catch this new skydiving custom job that Clevon Brooks is showing," Joe said.

"His planes are always worth seeing," Jamal remarked. "He usually comes up with some new twist. The one he's showing today is supposed to have some slick automated features."

"I wonder if that's the plane he was arguing with Grissom about," Joe said.

"Could be," Frank replied. "There's a spot down by the runway near the Cessna that should have a good view."

The three boys watched appreciatively as Brooks's custom blue-and-gold aircraft with the big hatch on the side rolled out onto the tarmac and headed for the runway.

"That's the plane we looked at on the first day," Frank commented.

"We'd better hurry if we want to see it take off," Joe said.

They cut between a couple of parked service vehicles and slid around an unmanned refueling truck.

"When they free up the airspace," Jamal said, "we should take another pass to look for my stolen plane again." He rubbed his hand through his short hair. "Man! This whole day has just been unreal!"

"And I think it just got weirder," Frank said, stopping suddenly.

Lying on the grass between the fuel truck and a parked plane was the body of Clevon Brooks.

7 Trouble in the Skies

Frank knelt beside the prone aviator and felt for a pulse. "He's just unconscious," he said.

"But if Brooks is here," Jamal said, kneeling next to Frank, "who's flying his plane?" Both of them glanced to where Brooks's custom aircraft was heading for the runway.

"Let's find out," Joe said, sprinting toward the taxiing plane.

"Call the cops," Frank said to Jamal as he rose and dashed after his brother.

The Hardys raced after the moving plane. It turned on the taxiway and headed for the runway. A startled cry rose from the crowd as the brothers sprinted toward the aircraft. Joe and Frank couldn't tell if the person flying the plane heard the shouts or if he knew the Hardys were chasing him.

Brooks's customized skydiving plane reached the end of the runway and revved its engine for takeoff. Then it began to roll down the aging concrete, gaining speed as it went.

Joe dashed forward and ducked under the tail's horizontal stabilizer, aiming for the rear door on the plane's right side. He knew Frank was right behind him, but the aircraft was picking up speed, and he couldn't wait for his brother to catch up.

The younger Hardy grabbed on to the door handle of the rear hatch. The motion of the plane nearly pulled his arm from its socket, but he held on. The momentum yanked his feet up off the ground, and the toes of his shoes skidded over the patched concrete for a moment.

Joe pulled himself forward and pushed off the ground with his feet. His legs shot out in front of him and dangled wildly in the air for a moment. He twisted and managed to get his feet onto the fiberglass fairing covering one of the rear wheels. He clung there precariously, trying to pull the door open.

Frank sprinted under the tail and toward Joe. He was close now, but the plane's speed was picking up fast. Joe extended his free hand toward Frank, but the elder Hardy was too far away.

The plane lurched slightly as it hit a bump in

the runway, and its wheels left the ground. Joe tightened his grip on the rear cargo door to avoid falling off.

Frank made one final, desperate leap to catch his brother. He came up inches short and fell hard onto the tarmac.

Clevon Brooks's stolen aircraft lifted into the air, taking Joe with it. The younger Hardy clung to the side of the plane, his hands on the door handle and his feet on the wheel cover. As the aircraft climbed higher and higher, he struggled with the door.

Finally, Joe managed to wrest the back door open and, without looking down, pull himself into the rear of the stolen plane.

Panting for breath, he looked up just as a ski-masked figure charged at him.

Frank picked himself up off the concrete. The crowd roared with surprise at the unexpected stunt; they didn't realize it wasn't part of the act. The security guards and police knew, though, and Frank heard their sirens approaching.

He heard something else as well: an airplane prop, getting louder by the second.

Frank turned to see the old Hawkins Cessna barreling down the runway toward him. Jamal was at the yobe and had left the copilot's door open. He motioned for Frank to hop aboard.

The elder Hardy gauged his timing and jumped as the Cessna rolled past. He caught hold of the doorframe and pulled himself into the copilot's chair.

"Buckle up," Jamal said. "We're going after that guy."

"Good thinking," Frank replied, doing as Jamal said. "Where's Brooks?"

"I left him with the EMTs," Jamal said.

He pulled back on the yobe, and the Cessna 182 flew up into the air.

"Think you can catch Brooks's plane?" Frank asked.

Jamal shrugged. "Depends on how skilled the pilot flying it is. We've got a chance, though."

Frank and Jamal watched as Joe pulled himself inside Brook's plane. Frank let out a sigh of relief.

"Maybe Joe will be able to take the guy out," Jamal said.

"Let's hope so," Frank replied. "Then maybe we can find your plane and wrap this case up."

"You think there's a connection between Brooks's plane being stolen and ours being stolen?"

Frank nodded. "Clearly something strange is going on at Scott Field. We've had a break-in, two stolen planes, a fist fight, and a crash, all within a day. The question is: What's the connection between all this?"

Joe got to his feet just in time; the masked thief was trying to push him out of the open door. Joe dodged out of the way and yanked the door shut behind him.

The thief clouted Joe on the jaw and forced him to reel back. His head hit the wood paneling on the rear bulkhead. Lights flashed before his eyes, but he recovered in time to block the masked man's follow-up blow.

Joe hammered his fist into the guy's belly. The thief swung as he doubled over, but Joe side-stepped past the blow.

The interior of Brooks's plane had an open floor plan. There were two doors in the rear: the cargo hatch that Joe had come through and a wide door on the opposite side of the plane. The stowage rack opposite the big door had several parachutes in it.

Six leather seats, similar to those in the stolen Hawkins plane, lined both walls. Two wood-paneled partitions separated the pilot from the rear of the plane. Joe saw someone moving beyond the partitions but couldn't get a good look at who it was.

"So, there are two of you," Joe said to the winded thief.

The bandit didn't reply but came at Joe again. He threw a haymaker at Joe's head. The younger Hardy ducked and counterpunched, landing a one, two combination on the thief's jaw. The criminal staggered back into the rack of parachutes.

Joe smiled and stepped toward the stunned enemy.

Suddenly the plane dipped to the side, and Joe fell back against the big jump door. A mechanical whir filled the cabin. The door Joe was pinned against began to open.

Frank and Jamal set their sights on the larger plane.

"Whoever's flying that thing's no ace," Jamal said.

"Lucky for us," Frank replied.

They'd been slowly gaining on the aircraft but hadn't managed to come alongside it yet. Jamal had kept in touch via radio with the Scott Field control tower. The authorities seemed none too pleased with Jamal's sudden departure, but there was little they could do about it.

"The theft of Brooks's airplane will probably keep them from coming down on us too hard," Frank said.

"Let's hope," Jamal replied. "All I need is *more* trouble. Man, am I gonna have a story or two for my father when he gets back."

"Here's wishing those stories have happy endings," Frank said grimly.

Jamal nodded. "Hey, I think I see someone struggling inside the aft cabin." He and Frank peered intently at the windows near the rear of the stolen plane.

"You're right," Frank said. "That would explain why Joe hasn't overpowered the pilot yet." He clenched his jaw. "If only I'd gotten aboard with him!"

"I bet Joe's thinking the same thing right now," Jamal said.

The stolen plane quickly veered to the left, and Jamal had to move quickly to keep up.

The thief Joe was fighting grabbed on to the parachute rack to avoid falling. He laughed as the door behind Joe slowly slid open.

Joe rolled aside, grasped the jump handle next to the door, and hung on for dear life. He pulled himself out of harm's way just as the door opened completely.

The black-masked thief seemed none too secure in his own position. He hung precariously from the parachute rack, his feet dangling toward the open door. The pilot must have sensed his comrade's distress, though, for the blue-and-gold plane suddenly straightened out.

The thief let go of the rack and grabbed the straps of one of the parachutes. He came at Joe, swinging the parachute like a weapon. Joe ducked the blow, but the felon caught him on the backswing.

Joe lashed out with his hands, grabbing the parachute's canvas cover to steady himself and keep from toppling out the open door.

Just then the stolen plane hit an air pocket and lurched. Joe and the masked thief tumbled across the deck, out the open door, and into the autumn sky.

8 The Long Fall

Frank's heart jumped into his throat as he saw his brother fall out the jump door of the stolen plane.

"Oh, man!" Jamal gasped.

"Keep the plane level!" Frank called. He unbuckled himself and dived over the back of the seat into the rear of the Cessna. He yanked frantically on something stowed under the plane's seats.

"What are you doing?" Jamal asked, a note of panic in his voice.

"I'm going after him," Frank said. He emerged with a parachute clutched in each hand.

"That's crazy," Jamal said, "but I'd do the same if it were my brother. Get going!"

Frank opened the plane's passenger door and,

checking to make sure he wouldn't hit the wing struts or the tail, jumped out.

Joe and the masked thief plummeted through the sky, each clinging desperately to the straps of their shared parachute.

The felon twisted in the air, pulling hard, trying to yank the chute from Joe's grip.

"Cut it out!" Joe yelled, unsure if the thief could hear him. "We can get out of this if we work together!"

The thief only fought harder. Joe struggled toward him through the air, fighting the rushing of the wind. He reached for the felon's hand. As he did, the thief spun around and kicked him.

Joe lost his grip on the parachute. The thief, struggling to put on the parachute, quickly drifted away from him.

Joe looked down. The ground was still a long way off.

Cold wind whipped against Frank Hardy as he struggled to put on one of the parachutes with his hands. He could see Joe and the thief tumbling through the air far ahead of him.

Suddenly the thief broke free from Joe, and the two separated. In his hand the thief clutched the pair's sole parachute.

For a moment Frank's concern for his brother nearly overwhelmed him. His concentration lapsed, and the wind ripped the second parachute from his hand. Frank watched helplessly as it sailed away into the clouds.

A moment later he saw the thief's parachute open above him, while Joe continued to free-fall through the air.

Frank fastened the remaining chute around his body and dived after his brother.

Joe forced himself not to panic. He'd been in some tight spots before, but this was certainly one of the worst. He called to mind all the things he'd learned when he first started skydiving. None of them seemed pertinent to jumping out of a plane without a parachute.

He knew he could control his descent by splaying his body in the air. He lay flat, parallel to the onrushing earth, and stretched his arms and legs out on both sides. This increased his wind resistance and slowed him down slightly—but not enough to keep him from being killed at the end of the fall. The air around him was bitterly cold. It chilled him right through his clothing.

The chances of living through a jump without a working chute were very small. The stories Joe remembered of people surviving such a plunge all involved a soft landing. He began looking around for something to land on that might merely break some bones rather than kill him.

Lakes and ponds were out of the question. Even during the summer, falling into one from this height would be like hitting a brick wall. There was a big lake almost directly below him, but it was frozen and covered with a fine sheen of snow.

A big snowdrift might cushion his fall, but there hadn't been enough snowfall yet to form anything suitable. Trees were the next best option, but most of the trees in the area had lost their leaves and looked more like spikes than a soft pile to jump into. Pine trees seemed little better.

The weather was too cold to find a good patch of mud or a newly plowed field. Joe gritted his teeth and shook his head in frustration. He had no good options.

A distant buzz drifted to his ears. He looked ahead and saw Jamal's plane circling ahead of him. Joe remembered once seeing a movie stunt, where a sky diver had landed on a moving plane. Jamal was too far away to try it, though. Despite this, the younger Hardy felt glad that his friend and his brother hadn't given up on him yet.

A shout pierced the chilly air. "Joe!"

Joe's heart raced as he turned his head and saw Frank plummeting toward him. The elder Hardy had tucked his arms to his side and was holding his legs tight and straight, making his body less wind-resistant. He shot forward rapidly, like a hawk diving out of the sky onto its pray.

In seconds he'd closed the distance between him and Joe.

Frank floated alongside his brother, and the two clasped hands. The icy ground below them was rushing up very quickly now.

"Just like buddy diving in the school pool when we were little!" Frank hollered.

Joe nodded and twisted his body in the air. Frank came in facing his brother and clasped his arms under Joe's arms. Joe wriggled his arms through some of the chute's restraints and locked his fingers together around Frank's back, making sure not to interfere with the parachute.

"Ready!" Joe said, shouting to be heard over the howling wind.

Frank pulled the ripcord, and the parachute shot into the sky. The round patch of nylon billowed open, and the brothers jerked hard as the chute slowed them down. Joe almost lost his grip, but Frank held on tightly.

The two of them slowly spiraled down toward the big frozen lake below. Tall pine trees lined the lakeshore. Long tracks, probably from snowmobiles, crossed the far end of the lake, miles away. A bit of rusty green prefab barn shone through the trees in that direction as well.

The snow-covered ice below them looked solid

enough. "Hang on!" Frank said, and he and Joe braced themselves for touchdown.

They hit hard and tumbled onto the ice. It wasn't a controlled roll, as they'd been taught in their parachuting lessons, but it was enough to blunt the impact. A big cracking sound echoed around them, but the ice held.

Frank moaned. Joe had landed on top of him.

"Man!" Joe said. "I don't think I've ever been more glad to see you, Frank!"

"Same here, little brother," Frank replied. "But would you mind getting off me? You weigh a ton."

Joe laughed and untangled himself from Frank's parachute harness. He rolled to one side and lay on the ice. "I ache all over!" he said.

"It beats being *spread* all over," Frank said.

"By a long shot," Joe replied. "Thanks—a lot."

"Don't mention it."

A buzzing overhead caught their attention, and they looked up to see Jamal circling the lake. Clouds had closed in overhead, and a cold fog seemed about to swallow the tiny Cessna.

"Feel up to waving?" Joe asked. They both were still lying flat on the ice.

"I'll just call him on the cell phone," Frank said. He dug into his jacket pocket and punched up Jamal's number, then hit the speakerphone button on the handset. "Jamal?" Frank asked.

"Boy, am I glad to hear you!" Jamal's voice blared.

There was some interference in the signal, but they could make out his words well enough. "Are you both okay?"

"Battered and bruised, but still here," Joe replied.

"Phew!" Jamal said. "I was sure you were both goners. I'm trying to find a place to land, but I don't know that the ice will support the plane."

"I wouldn't chance it," Frank said. "It gave a pretty good crack when we landed."

"I'm sure it's still patchy in spots," Joe said. "The weather hasn't been cold enough yet to form a really thick sheet."

"I'll keep looking," Jamal said, "but the weather's closing in up here." His last words were almost drowned in static.

"We're losing you," Frank said. "I thought I saw a barn on the far side of the lake before we landed. We'll try to make for it."

"Get back to the airport and send a search party," Joe said. "No sense your crashing trying to save us."

"Roger," Jamal said. "I'll talk to you—" Static swallowed the remainder of his message.

The brothers tried for a few more moments to get him back, but with no success.

"We must be right at the edge of cell range," Frank said.

"And the weather's cutting us off from the local relay tower," Joe replied. "I'm glad we got Jamal, though. The Global Positioning System in his plane will make it easier for a search party to find us."

"Let's get off this ice," Frank said. "I'm freezing."

He and Joe stood slowly and gathered up their parachute. They repacked it onto Frank's back and then made their way toward the edge of the lake.

"We'll follow the lakeshore up to where I saw that rusty barn," Frank said.

"Good plan," Joe said. "Let's hope that whatever farmhouse the barn belongs to isn't deserted."

Frank nodded. "It sure would be nice to get back to a warm bed tonight."

"Or a semiwarm sleeping bag," Joe told him.

"Hmm," Frank said. "Maybe we should spring for a hotel room after all."

"Let's get back to civilization first."

They skidded across the snow-frosted ice toward a nearby pine-covered peninsula. The clouds descended further as they walked, and soon the distance became lost in a gray fog.

"The weather's caught between fall and winter," Joe said. "I guess we should be happy it's not snowing."

"I'll be happy—"

Frank was cut off by a large cracking sound. Suddenly the ice gave way beneath his feet, and he plunged into the dark waters below.

9 The Ghost in the Ice

"Frank!" Joe yelled. He dropped onto all fours to prevent the ice from breaking beneath him and scrambled toward the edge of the hole. When he peered into the water, though, he saw no sign of his brother.

Frank Hardy plunged into the chilly deep. The parachute on his back became waterlogged almost instantly. The heavy backpack dragged him down toward the lake's unknown depths.

Frank pulled the parachute pack from his back and let it fall to the bottom. The water felt like cold needles piercing his skin. He glanced up and saw a broken circle of light above, the hole through which he had fallen.

Then something closer by caught his eye. It was an aircraft, an airplane submerged beneath the ice, half buried in the bottom of the lake. The craft's dark red tail jutted up from the murky waters below. It seemed about the same shape and size as one of the Sullivan Brothers custom airplanes. Curiosity rose in Frank's brain, but he didn't have enough air in his lungs to take a long look.

Kicking hard, he shot toward the pale light above. He broke surface next to Joe's extended hands. The younger Hardy grabbed his brother by the arms and pulled. Frank scrambled up, and a few moments later the two lay on the ice side by side, panting.

"Glad you came up," Joe said. "I thought for a moment that I'd have to dive in after you."

"Me too," Frank said.

"How long do you think it will take to crawl to shore?" Joe asked. "Or do you want to chance walking again?"

"No thanks," Frank said. "I'll be pretty frozen by the time we get there, but I think I prefer being a Popsicle to falling in again."

"Let's go then."

Cautiously they crept the thirty yards from the hole in the ice to the wooded shore of the peninsula.

"How far do you think it is to that barn?" Joe asked.

"At least two or three miles," Frank said. "We won't make it before dark."

"We'd better dry you off then," Joe said. "I could stand to warm up too. Next time I go parachuting, remind me to take my jumpsuit."

"The next time I go swimming under the ice, remind me to take my wet suit," Frank replied. "Come on, let's see if we can get a fire started."

They cleared a bare patch on the ground at the edge of the pine forest. Fortunately there was little snow to move away, and what there was consisted mostly of light powder. They found plenty of dry pine needles in the woods to use as tinder and enough stout sticks and dead branches to make a good stack.

Utilizing their knowledge from years of scout camp, the brothers quickly got a small blaze going, which they soon built into a good-size fire. Frank dangled his clothes, piece by piece, on sticks over the fire until they were dry. Joe was soon feeling toasty as well.

"This is a little more *extreme* camping than I'd intended when I came along on this trip," Joe said.

"This is a little more extreme *everything* than I intended when I came along," Frank replied. "Two plane thefts, a break-in, a fistfight, a crash, and some skydiving and swimming to top it all off."

"I'm glad I didn't join you on that last part," Joe said, rubbing his fingers together to warm them.

"I'm glad you didn't too. One Hardy-sicle in the family is enou—" Frank stopped in midword and slapped his palm to his forehead. "I almost forgot. . . . You won't believe what I saw down there under the ice."

"What?"

"An airplane," Frank said. "A maroon-tailed airplane."

"The stolen Hawkins plane?" Joe asked.

"That's what I thought at first," Frank replied, "but now I'm not so sure. Do you remember the serial numbers on the tail of the stolen plane?"

Joe thought a moment. "R-U-four-seven-eight . . . something. There was one more number," he said.

"Four. That's what I remember too," Frank said. "But those aren't the numbers on the tail of the plane I saw. It was hard to tell, since I was freezing and drowning at the time, but I think the numbers on the plane under the ice were S-T-three-eight-seven-eight."

"Was it a Sullivan custom plane you saw?" Joe asked.

"I didn't get a very good look at it," Frank replied. "I thought it was, though."

"You'll excuse me if I don't go check and give you a second opinion," Joe said, winking.

Frank nodded.

Joe ran one hand through his hair. "It doesn't make any sense. Why would there be an airplane sunk at the bottom of a lake out here in Kendall State Park? And why would that plane be the same make and color as the plane that was stolen from Jamal last night?"

"It's a mystery, all right," Frank said, smiling.

"We'll have some experience with sleeping on the ground if we don't get going," Joe said, changing the subject. "If you're dry enough, we should douse this fire and head for that barn."

"Good idea. First, let's make some torches, if we can. I forgot to bring my flashlight along on this trip, and I'm betting you did too."

"Must have left it with my parachute," Joe said with an ironic grin. "I've got my pocketknife, though."

"Me too," said Frank.

The brothers managed to pull together enough pine needles, dry twigs, and grasses to make one decent torch head. They combined these ingredients with strips torn from their undershirts and some pine pitch they tapped from a tree with their pocketknives.

It was after nightfall by the time they completed their task and finally doused the fire. The fog had crept in on them in that time, and the whole world looked like dark gray cotton when they finally set out for the distant barn.

"Some of those snowmobile tracks look like they lead to something closer," Frank said. "Maybe we should try to follow them instead. They did head out over the lake, though."

"Let's not get any more impromptu swimming

practice if we can avoid it," Joe replied.

Frank nodded, and they stuck to the shore. The going was difficult. Rocks and fallen trees littered the shoreline, and tangled roots sprang suddenly out of the fog, grabbing their sneakers.

As night deepened, the fog grew thicker. It clung to the brothers' clothing, making the Hardys feel ever colder and more damp than before.

"That shortcut across the lake isn't sounding too bad right now," Joe said, his teeth chattering.

"No," Frank replied. "You were right. Falling in again would be about the worst thing we could do. On the shore we can make another fire if we get too cold and tired."

Joe looked up at their makeshift torch, flickering in his hand. "If we're going to stop to make another fire, we should do it soon," he said. "This torch may not last much longer, and it won't be easy to light a new fire in this damp fog."

"Let's press on a little farther," Frank said. "We ought to be getting close to that barn."

A loud crack echoed through the woods.

"Was that the ice?" Joe asked.

Another crack, and the torch flew out of Joe's hand.

"Sniper!" Frank yelled, diving for cover.

Joe hit the snow-dappled ground and rolled behind a big pine tree. "Where is he?" the younger Hardy asked. "Can you see him?"

"Ahead of us, I think," Frank replied from his position behind a nearby rock. "It's hard to tell in this fog. I'm surprised he can see us at all."

Crack! Another shot whizzed over their heads.

"We'd be sitting ducks if we headed onto the ice," Joe said. "We'll have to go back."

"Or deeper into the woods," Frank said. He gathered a small pile of snow into his hands and made a snowball. "I'm going to throw this toward where the shots are coming from. When I do, head for the tall timber as fast as you can."

"Check," Joe said.

Frank ducked out from behind the rock and lobbed the snowball. Simultaneously Joe sprinted from behind the tree, heading inland.

Crack! A shot whizzed by Frank. The elder Hardy bolted, following his brother.

"You think it's that guy from the plane?" Joe asked as they ran.

"The skydiver?" Frank said. "Probably. I don't know who else it could be." He jumped over a fallen log and nearly lost his footing. Another shot whizzed over the brothers' heads. They kept running.

"A disgruntled landowner maybe," Joe said. "Or maybe the pilot of the plane. Did you see if it landed after I fell out?"

"I was too busy worrying about you!"

"Hey, heads up!" Joe called.

Frank ducked, barely avoiding a hanging tree

branch in their way. They began running downhill, through low brush and powder snow. Pine needles and dead leaves skidded from under their sneakers, and they struggled to stay on their feet.

They heard another gunshot, but didn't hear the bullet hit anything this time.

"Maybe we're losing him," Joe said.

"Let's hope," Frank replied.

"Any idea which way we're headed?"

"East, more or less," Frank said. "Assuming I haven't lost track of where the lake is."

"I think I could lose track of anything in this fog," Joe said. "We're not getting any nearer to the rescue site either."

Frank shook his head. "I know. It'll be a wonder if they find us, if this sniper doesn't find us first."

"Do you hear something?" Joe asked. "Like wind blowing through the leaves?"

They didn't dare stop, but both brothers concentrated as they ran. A sound was steadily building ahead of them. A muffled roar filled the air, as if a strong rainstorm were approaching through the forest.

They broke through the edge of the woods and onto a rocky slope. Joe stabbed his hand out and grabbed Frank by the shoulder, just before the elder Hardy toppled down a rocky embankment. At the bottom of the slope a swift-running river surged downhill.

"Dead end!" Joe said.

The river was wide—too wide to jump or ford—and more treacherous than any stretch of white water the brothers had ever navigated.

They looked both up and down the river as far as the fog allowed, but they saw no easy way to cross.

Crack! Another shot whizzed over their heads.

"If we stay here," Frank hissed, "we're sitting ducks!"

With a silent nod of agreement, both brothers jumped off the embankment toward the raging river below.

10 Ice Man

The Hardys hurtled through the air, over the intervening rocks, and into the frigid waters.

The river surged around them, trying to drag them under. Joe returned to the surface first. A moment later Frank's head popped up. They swirled downstream amid huge boulders and dangerous white water.

They swam with all their might, trying to stay away from the big rocks and dangerous eddies that might suck them below the surface. Joe got turned around but righted himself just in time to avoid hitting his head on a stony outcropping. Instead he hit the boulder with his leg and grunted in pain. "Man!" he said. "I *told* you I didn't want to go swimming today."

Frank would have laughed, but just then a wave splashed over his head and into his mouth. He coughed the water out and kept paddling downstream.

Another shot rang out—this time far away. Neither brother heard the bullet whiz by since the roaring of the river made it almost impossible to hear anything.

The water was freezing, and the brothers were quickly losing their ability to swim in it.

"We need . . . to get out!" Frank said, barely keeping his head above the white water.

"First chance . . . we get," Joe replied.

They looked for a shoal, but none presented itself. The banks of the river had grown higher, becoming something like a small canyon. Tall rocks lined the shores, and the clinging fog made it difficult to see anything beyond them.

"W-What's that up ahead?" Joe called, pointing toward a dark shape looming before them in the river.

Frank peered at the vaguely rectangular shape that jutted out over the swirling waters.

"A bridge!" he said. "Try to g-grab one of the pylons!"

"As if y-you had to tell me," Joe replied.

The water near the right side of the bridge seemed more calm and less treacherous, so both brothers aimed for there.

As they drew closer, they saw that the bridge was built from big logs—like telephone poles—expertly joined together with metal bolts. Its pylons were anchored on concrete pads, set at the edge of the waterline.

Joe and Frank kicked as hard as they could, but the water kept trying to pull them back toward the center of the river. They heaved up over a big submerged rock, and, with one final surge, grabbed on to the cement base of the nearest pylon.

The water pressure was terrific and threatened to pull them off the concrete and hurl them downstream once more. Ever so slowly they dragged themselves around the side of the pad and onto the rocky shore at the bottom of the bridge.

Exhausted and chilled to the bone, Frank and Joe lay there for a moment. They tried to recover their breaths.

"Man," Joe said, shivering, "that was like a water park ride gone bad."

"I wouldn't want to try it again," Frank said, "even in the summer. Even in a kayak."

"I hear that," Joe replied.

They rested another few moments, then wrung out their clothes as best they could. Slowly they climbed up the slope to the bridge.

"Thank heaven for the park service," Frank said, gazing at the well-tended trail leading in either direction.

"If I remember the big area map I studied on our way to the show," Joe said, "the river through the park runs north and south. There's an entrance to the park on the west—"

"And another on the south," Frank said, "but I agree that we're probably closer to the western one."

"So we should go this way to find civilization— and heat," Joe said, indicating the trail leading away from the bridge on the side they were standing on.

"I agree," Frank said. "Let's get going. It won't be getting any warmer tonight."

Joe nodded, and the two of them jogged down the trail into the fog-shrouded forest.

They tried Frank's cell phone, but two dunkings with a trip down the rapids had made it useless. Building a fire seemed out of the question as well. The only thing to do was to keep moving and hope to build up their body heat.

Three-quarters of an hour later the trail crossed a pitted dirt road.

"What do you think?" Frank asked.

"Roads have to have traffic," Joe said, "or at least lead to civilization."

"North or south, then?"

"Jewel Ridge and Scottsville are to the south," Joe pointed out.

"South it is," Frank said.

The fog cleared a bit as they jogged down the road. Soon they could make out the dim shapes of the hills and trees ahead. However, they saw no buildings or other signs of civilization.

About a half hour later, a sound drifted through the fog.

"A car engine!" Joe said. For a moment excitement flashed across his face, quickly followed by a look of concern. "Do you think it's the sniper?"

Frank shook his head. "If it is, he found a way to skirt around us and come back from the opposite direction where we last saw him."

"It's possible," Joe said.

"Yeah. I guess it is."

"Let's put an obstruction across the road," Joe suggested. "That way whoever it is will have to stop, and if the person has a gun or any weapons, we can hold him."

"Sounds like a plan," Frank said. "I'd be more than happy to pay that guy back for what he put us through."

The brothers quickly searched the brush on either side of the road. In no time Joe located a big rotting log. The two of them hauled it out of the woods and dropped it across the dirt road. They picked up a couple of stout branches to use as weapons and took up positions on either side of the rutted track. The boys chose concealed spots close to the road. That way, when the car stopped and the shooter got out, they'd be able to jump him from behind.

They tried not to shiver as they waited for the approaching vehicle.

The green-and-brown four-by-four roared out of the fog. The driver spotted the big log laid across the road and skidded the vehicle to a halt. He got out to look at the blockage. The man was dressed in a tan park ranger's uniform and hat.

The Hardys came out of the woods and hailed the man. They held on to their sticks, since they'd never gotten a good look at the sniper. It seemed unlikely that this ranger would be the shooter, but . . .

"Hey!" Joe said. "Are you with the park service?"

The driver turned, surprised to see them. The brothers noticed that he wasn't wearing a sidearm and surreptitiously dropped their sticks. The ranger peered at them through the fog and darkness.

"Are you Frank and Joe Hardy?" the man asked.

The brothers exchanged a puzzled glance. "That's us," Frank said.

The ranger smiled. "I was sent out to look for you boys," he said, "but they told me you'd be out by Lake Kendall. How'd you get this far south?"

"That's a long, wet story," Frank said.

"We'd be happy to tell you once we're in a nice, warm car, though," Joe added.

"Hop in," the ranger said. "I'll get some blankets out of the back."

The brothers helped the ranger move the big log out of the road, then the three of them got into the

Jeep. The ranger grabbed some blankets from the back of the four-by-four. The brothers huddled together as the ranger turned up the heat inside the vehicle.

"That was pretty clever, putting that log across the road to get me to stop," the ranger said. "You guys must be pretty resourceful. To tell you the truth, I'm surprised to find you alive. They told me that you jumped out of a plane, and one of you didn't have a parachute."

"Two planes, actually," Joe said.

"We were chasing some airplane thieves," Frank said, "but they got away."

"They stole a plane belonging to one of our friends," Joe added.

"Out at Scott Field," the ranger said, nodding. "I heard about that on the news. They said the plane stolen this afternoon disappeared over the park."

"Have there been any other planes that disappeared over the park before?" Frank asked.

"You mean aside from the one stolen last night?" the ranger asked. "Not that I've heard."

"We were thinking of sometime earlier—this year or maybe last," Joe explained. "Maybe even longer ago than that."

"Not that I'm aware of," the ranger said, "and I've been working here for five years. Why do you ask?"

Joe and Frank exchanged furtive glances and decided not to mention the plane under the ice at the moment. "No reason," Frank said. "We're just trying to see if there's a pattern here."

"Could we use your cell phone?" Frank then asked, noting one plugged into the cigarette lighter next to the Jeep's two-way radio.

"Be my guest," the ranger said. "The reception is pretty spotty out here, but I think we're close enough to the relay tower for it to work all right. Help yourself. I'm going to call in the news that I found you and you're okay." He handed Frank the cell phone and picked up the two-way radio receiver for himself.

The ranger called into park headquarters while Frank dialed Jamal. The brothers arranged to have Jamal pick them up; the ranger called off the search-and-rescue operation that had been sent out to find the boys. The brothers then called their parents to let them know that they were okay.

"Jamal's renting a car," Frank told Joe. "He'll meet us at the ranger station at the southern edge of the park."

"I told the search-and-rescue guys to keep the media away," the ranger said. "I figure you guys have gone through enough for one day."

"Definitely!" Joe exclaimed.

In half an hour they arrived at the ranger station. Jamal showed up soon after that. He'd brought a fresh change of clothes for the brothers, who were more than glad to get out of their wet clothes.

"So, you told the rangers about the sniper in the woods," Jamal said.

"We said that we thought someone was shooting at us," Frank replied.

"They said that the property on the north side of the lake was private land and out of their jurisdiction, but they'd look into it," Joe added. "They're checking for the other parachutist too. But I doubt they'll find him. It's a pretty big area to search."

"They seemed to think the shooter might have been a hunter who mistook us for a game animal in the dark," said Frank.

"You guys don't think so, though," Jamal said.

"The person with the gun chased us," Joe said. "You might fire one shot at a shape in the darkness by mistake, but not a half dozen."

"So, do you think it was the parachutist?" Jamal asked.

Joe shook his head. "If that guy had a weapon handy, why did he attack me with a parachute?"

"Maybe he had an accomplice on the ground," Frank said.

"Maybe they landed the plane nearby and came after you," Jamal suggested.

"Could be," Joe said, "though we didn't see the plane land in the fog."

"Hang on," Frank said. "The tracks we saw on the ice might have been from a plane, right?"

"It'd be pretty risky landing on that ice," Jamal said.

"But they'd need to pick up the second hijacker," Joe said. "And shooting us might seem a good idea to the thieves—to get rid of witnesses."

"It still doesn't explain where the gun came from," Frank said, "unless the pilot had it in the cockpit."

"Criminals have been known to carry weapons," Jamal said, a hint of sarcasm in his voice.

Three quarters of an hour later they arrived back at Scott Field. The night was pitch-black. Patches of fog still limited visibility at the airfield. Jamal had borrowed the car he was using from Elise; arranging to rent one would have taken too much time.

"She was really glad you guys were okay," Jamal said as he pulled the car into the administration building parking lot. "This whole thing really has her flustered." They parked the car and got out. "She said I should slip the car keys through the mail slot in the door. She was going home to try to get some rest."

"All the trouble with the show must be pretty stressful," Joe said.

"I think she used the words 'worst nightmare,'" Jamal said. He pushed the keys through the mail slot of the building. Frank checked the door, just to make sure it hadn't been taped open again. It hadn't.

"I'm surprised the whole airfield isn't crawling with police and reporters," Frank said.

"It was earlier, but you know how those media vultures are," Jamal said. "They move on if there's no fresh meat to circle."

"Cops and investigators need sleep too, I guess," Joe commented.

"I'm sure they'll be back in force tomorrow morning," Frank said. They cut around the building and headed toward the Cessna; Jamal wanted to check it one more time before they turned in.

As they passed by the old control tower, Joe stopped suddenly. "Look!" he said.

A shadowy figure was moving around in the darkened room at the top of the tower.

11 Tower of Peril

"Let's check it out," Frank said. The three friends tried the door at the base of the control tower. It was open.

"Taped, just like the door to Flaubert's office," Joe said.

"These guys need to get some new tricks," Jamal whispered.

"Sometimes the old tricks are the best," Frank said.

They crept into the base of the tower, which appeared to be mostly storage space for spare parts and other items connected to the maintenance of the tower and its equipment.

Finding the stairs, they moved quickly up to the second floor, which housed the electronic guts of the control tower operations. The stairs from the second floor wound up one wall of the tower to the third-floor control deck. As silently as they could the teens ran up into the control room.

As they topped the stairs, they saw a black-garbed figure bent over one of the radar control panels at the far side of the room. The computer beside the panel was on, and the intruder seemed to be working at the keyboard. The black ski mask pulled over his head was proof—as if the taped door weren't enough—that he was *not* part of the regular air traffic crew.

When he heard the boys' footsteps, the surprised opponent rose quickly and flicked the computer's off switch. He turned as the teens ran at him. By the time Frank got to him, the burglar was ready.

The masked man kicked the chair he had been sitting on at the group. It shot across the floor on its metal wheels and caught Frank and Joe in the legs.

As they staggered, the criminal grabbed a folding chair stacked against the wall nearby. He swung the chair into Frank's back, and the elder Hardy crashed to the floor. The burglar tried to catch Joe on the backswing, but the younger Hardy seized the chair and shoved hard.

The burglar stumbled back across the room. Joe tried to pin the intruder against the wall with the chair. The burglar dropped suddenly and swept his left leg into Joe's knees. Joe fell back, hard, but Jamal rushed in to take his place.

Jamal jabbed with his left, then aimed for the burglar's chin with a right uppercut. The intruder countered the first blow, but couldn't entirely deflect the second. Jamal's fist caught him on the jaw. The burglar staggered back into the glass door leading onto the balcony.

As the Hardys got to their feet, Jamal bore in on their enemy. The burglar opened the door behind him and stepped out onto the mesh floor of the balcony. Jamal rushed onto the narrow walkway after him.

The burglar kept backing up, drawing Jamal farther around the balcony.

"Keep him pinned, Jamal!" Joe called as he and Frank rushed through the door after him. "We'll circle behind!"

"Got it," Jamal said, aiming another punch at the intruder's head. The felon blocked the blow. Frank and Joe ran to the other side of the balcony to take him from the back.

When Jamal threw his next punch, the burglar blocked it and surged forward. He snapped his forehead into Jamal's face, head-butting him. Jamal staggered back, and the intruder shoved him hard.

Jamal toppled over the balcony railing, barely grabbing hold of the steel rail as he went. He hung over the edge, his feet dangling in the air.

The intruder dashed past Jamal and back into the control tower.

"Jamal!" Joe cried as he and Frank raced to his rescue.

The brothers grabbed hold of their friend's arms and quickly hauled him back up to the balcony. As they did so, the burglar ran down the stairs and out of the control tower.

"Thanks, guys," Jamal said. "Sorry I lost him." He looked dazed.

"We may catch him yet," Frank said. "Are you okay?"

"Still seeing spots in front of my eyes from when he head-butted me," Jamal said.

"Wait here," Joe said. "We'll catch the guy."

He and Frank tore through the control room and back down the stairs. When they exited the control tower, they saw no sign of the burglar.

"I think I saw him go toward the east row of hangars!" Jamal called down to them from the balcony above.

"Thanks!" Joe yelled back. He and Frank sprinted toward the hangars and soon caught sight of the figure. He was darting between the buildings up ahead.

"This time he's not giving us the slip," Frank said. He sped up, and Joe ran to keep up. They darted into the narrow walkway between the two hangars where the burglar had disappeared.

As the Hardys came out from behind the

buildings, a flash of movement to their right caught their attention. They thought it might be the burglar, but a moment later they spotted the guy up the alley, moving in the opposite direction. The brothers turned and ran after the man.

Before they had gone a dozen steps, though, a bloodcurdling scream split the damp air.

"Help! Help me!"

It was a woman's voice, and it was coming from the other side of the service buildings behind the hangars.

For a moment the brothers hesitated.

The frantic cry sounded again. "Help!"

"Let's go," Joe called to Frank. He turned and ran toward the scream. Grumbling, Frank did the same; he didn't want to lose the intruder.

They dashed between two of the cinder block support buildings and came out near the front of the cafeteria. As they emerged from the narrow alley, they saw a woman lying crumpled on the ground next to a large puddle of water.

"Are you all right?" Frank asked, rushing to the woman's side.

The woman raised her mud-covered face, and they saw it was Rita Davenport. "A man came out of the fog and attacked me!" she said.

"What did he look like?" Joe asked.

"He was wearing black clothes and had on a black mask," she said.

Frank scowled. "We knew the burglar had an accomplice," he said. "There were *two* people aboard Brooks's stolen plane. Did he hurt you?"

"I thought he was going to," Ms. Davenport said, "but no. He just knocked me down. I'll be all right. Just give me a minute."

"The two guys must have arranged to meet behind the hangar," Joe said. "When we chased the guy from the control tower, they split up."

"And one of them attacked Ms. Davenport," Frank said. "Possibly as a distraction." He helped the frightened woman to her feet.

"Whether they planned it or not, we've lost those guys now," Joe pointed out.

"W-Would you please walk me back to my motel room?" Ms. Davenport asked. "Or maybe Mr. Manetti's room. I just don't feel safe alone." She brushed her tangled blond hair away from her pretty face and looked at the brothers.

"Sure thing," Frank said. "We'll make sure you get back safely." He and Joe escorted Ms. Davenport back across the airfield to the old motel. As they walked, they heard police sirens approaching Scott Field.

"Looks like Jamal got in touch with the police," Frank said. "Too bad we don't have much for them."

"Helping Ms. Davenport was more important than catching that burglar," Joe told him. "I'd hate to think that anyone got hurt, even if we were chasing a criminal."

"Thanks again," Ms. Davenport said as they reached the motel. "Mr. Manetti is in room forty-two."

"No problem," Joe replied. "But I wonder, what were you doing prowling around the airfield so late at night?"

"I wanted something to drink, and the machine at the motel was all out of the soda I like," she replied. "I remembered that the machine near the cafeteria had the same brand, so I went there. It didn't seem like a dangerous idea at the time." She knocked on Manetti's door.

"Just a minute," a man's voice called from inside. A moment later Tony Manetti, dressed in a bathrobe, appeared at the door. His hair was wet, and he had a towel in his hand. "Rita?" he said. "What's going on?"

"A masked man jumped me near the cafeteria."

"That's awful," Manetti said. "Are you all right?"

"I'm fine," Davenport said. "I just need someplace safe to sit and relax awhile."

"Come on in," Manetti said. "You can stay as long as you need to. Just let me get dressed." Turning to the Hardys, he added, "Thanks for bringing her back to the motel."

"No problem," Frank said. Eyeing Manetti's wet

hair, he asked, "Where were you just a little while ago?"

"I was here, taking a shower, until you came," Manetti said. "Why do you ask?"

"I was with Mr. Manetti until I went for my soda," Davenport said. "We were talking about business possibilities at the air show tomorrow."

"If there *is* an air show tomorrow," Joe said. "With so much trouble, I wouldn't be surprised if it was canceled."

"Oh, I doubt that," Manetti said. "There are too many industry people meeting here. There's important business to be done. For a lot of folks this is a make-or-break show every year."

"Is it make or break for you?" Frank asked.

"Nah," Manetti said. "I try never to put all my eggs in one basket. Anyway, thanks again, boys. I'll take care of Rita now." She stepped inside, and Manetti closed the door.

"Come on," Frank said. "We'd better get back to Jamal." He and Joe looked back toward the control tower. The police cars were gathering around it.

As they began to walk in that direction, a voice called them. "Hey, boys, what's all the commotion about?" It was Jack Meeker. Dressed in jeans and a T-shirt, he stood in a motel room doorway.

"Yeah, what's going on?" growled Rock Grissom,

appearing in another doorway. He was dressed in a robe and was rubbing his eyes.

"A break-in at the control tower," Frank said.

"It seems to me that trouble must like you guys," Meeker said. "It seems to follow you everywhere."

"Isn't this motel a little low-class for you, Mr. Meeker?" Joe asked testily.

Meeker smiled. "I like to stay close to the action," he said. "Though I'll admit, there's more action here than I expected."

"Nothing to worry about," Frank said. "You should go back to bed."

"I won't have some kid telling me what to do," Grissom said. He went back into his room and emerged moments later dressed in black leather pants and his fleece-collared black aviator's jacket. "I'm going to check my plane," he grumbled, striding out onto the tarmac.

"Well," Meeker said, "never say I don't have more sense than Rock Grissom. Good night." He closed the door to his room, and a moment later his light went out.

Joe and Frank headed for the control tower. When they got there they found Jamal standing near the tower door, talking to several police officers. Elise Flaubert, looking as though she'd just been dragged out of bed, stood talking to another officer a short distance away.

"Are these your friends?" the lead officer asked Jamal as the Hardys walked up.

"Yeah, that's Frank and Joe," Jamal replied.

"Get in the back of the patrol car, boys," the officer said. "We're all going down to the station to talk over your involvement in these crimes."

12 The Legend of 878

"But we're *not* involved in these crimes," Joe said. "We've been trying to prevent them."

"Look, kid," the officer said, "all I know is that lately, whenever something odd happens at this airport, you kids are in the middle of it. So get in the patrol car and we'll all go down to the station and sort things out, understand?"

"Sure, Officer. No problem," Frank said, reluctantly giving in. He, Joe, and Jamal got into the back of the patrol car, and they all rode down to the police department.

The Scottsville station consisted of a single large room. There was a receptionist's desk up front, and a low wooden railing separated the public area from an area holding four metal desks, one for the head of the squad and the others for the on-duty officers. Another room in back had three cells for prisoners.

Though it was the middle of the night when they arrived, the station was buzzing with activity. Officers from all shifts were crowded into the room, shuffling papers, drinking coffee, and discussing the recent incidents at the airport. A tired-looking NTSB official glared suspiciously at the teens as they entered the room.

The brothers and Jamal spent the next three hours detailing everything that had gone on during the previous day and a half. They stuck to the facts, leaving out any speculation about how the pieces of this strange puzzle might fit together. They went over the theft of Hawkins Air's new plane, the break-in at the office, the hijacking of Brooks's custom sky jumper, the discovery of the sunken plane, the chase through the forest, and finally, the fight in the control tower.

In the end the police and detectives looked just as puzzled as the Hardys and Jamal felt. The authorities, however, didn't admit that they had no more idea of what was going on than the boys did.

The police talked about holding the Hardys on "suspicion." They seemed to believe that the brothers must be mixed up in the case somehow, despite Jamal's legitimate business reason for being at the airport.

The brothers used one of their permitted phone calls to talk to their father. Fenton Hardy contacted Con Riley, the brothers' friend in the Bayport Police Department, and Riley vouched for them. This seemed to placate the Scottsville police, though the safety board agent still seemed unconvinced.

Fenton Hardy seemed concerned about his sons and made them promise—for the peace of mind of their mother and their aunt Gertrude—to keep their noses clean with the police. The brothers declined Mr. Hardy's offer of assistance, though they did ask him to get in touch with Jamal's father; Jamal had still not been able to get through. Fenton Hardy promised to try, and the phone call ended with the hint that he'd be bringing them home himself if he heard any more reports of sky-diving without a parachute. The brothers promised to stay out of trouble.

Frank and Joe hung up the phone and exchanged looks of concern. Fenton Hardy, renowned detective, was not about to let them stay at the air show if they distressed their mother or aunt any further.

"We'll have to keep out of the public eye from now on," Frank said.

"That would be fine with me as well," said the Scottsville chief of police, a burly middle-aged man with a white mustache. "Now if you boys won't be needing my station phones anymore, maybe my men and I can get back to solving these crimes."

"Did you have any luck finding out about that sunken plane?" Joe asked.

"If we had any luck," said the NTSB man, poking his thin nose into the conversation, "it wouldn't be any concern of yours."

"You boys stay out of this from now on, understand?" the chief said.

The brothers nodded. "Yes, sir."

"It's nearly dawn," the chief said. "Go back to the airport, and get some sleep. You can go too, Hawkins."

"Thanks," Jamal said, rousing himself from a chair. None of the boys had gotten any sleep that night.

Clevon Brooks had walked into the station earlier and spent the last fifteen minutes speaking to a patrol officer about the disappearance of his plane. He didn't seem too pleased with what the officer was telling him. As the brothers and Jamal headed for the door, Brooks's conversation became louder.

"We're doing all we can, Mr. Brooks," the officer said.

"Well, it's not enough!" Brooks complained. "If I don't get that plane back before the end of this show, my business is going right down the tubes!"

"Honestly, Mr. Brooks," the NTSB investigator said, "everyone here is dedicated to recovering your plane, and the Hawkins plane, as quickly as possible."

Brooks looked around the crowded station, pure frustration on his face.

"We'll call you just as soon as we find anything," the chief of police said.

"If you find anything *before* my creditors disconnect my phone, you mean," Brooks said. He turned and left the police station. The Hardys and Jamal followed him out.

"Actually, Mr. Brooks, there may be something more you can do," Joe said.

"We're looking into the disappearance of the Hawkins plane," Frank added, "and we're sure the two thefts are connected to a plane we found sunken beneath the ice in Lake Kendall."

"It looked like another Sullivan Brothers custom job," Joe said. "The numbers on its tail were S-T-eight-seven-eight. You've been working with planes a long time. Is there anything you know about that particular Sullivan custom job?"

Brooks's eyes grew wide. "You found Sullivan custom eight-seven-eight?" he asked incredulously. "You're pulling my leg, right?"

The brothers and Jamal shook their heads earnestly.

"I thought everyone in the business knew that story," Brooks said. "Eight-seven-eight was stolen by Carl Denny. He was part of a gang that stole three million dollars' worth of rare coins from a museum in Newport, Rhode Island. The rest of the gang got caught and thrown in prison for five years, but Denny managed to slip away with the money.

"The police caught up with him later. They

112

found out he was working in the Sullivan Brothers Air Customizing shop in Albany. But Denny, who was calling himself Dennis Carlson, found out they were on to him the same night the police planned to raid his place. The cops chased him to the Sullivan shop, a big hangar in a tiny airport west of the city.

"Before they could catch him, Denny hot-wired one of the planes in the shop. He drove the plane out of the big display window onto the runway and took off. No one has ever seen him—or the plane—again," Brooks finished.

"What about the stolen coins?" Jamal asked.

"The police never found the money either," Brooks replied.

"That's interesting," Frank said, rubbing his head, "but I can't immediately see how that ties into the current thefts."

"You boys look exhausted," Brooks said. "Why don't I give you a lift to wherever you're staying?"

"We're in the campground by the airfield," Joe said.

"Perfect," Brooks replied. "I was going that way anyway. I've got something to discuss with Elise."

"Great," Frank said, "we'll probably think better after we've had some rest."

The three friends piled into Brooks's rental car. By the time the sun rose, they were back at the campground. They crawled into their sleeping bags without a complaint about the cold, cramped conditions and slept through the rest of the morning. They didn't even notice the hustle and bustle of the Fly By & Buy air show taking place on the runway beside the campground.

They finally got up in the afternoon, showered and shaved, and put on warm clothes and jackets. Then they hauled themselves over to the cafeteria for a very late brunch.

"Well, if it's not the prodigal troublemakers," Jack Meeker declared as they entered the room. He and a number of other attendees, including Rock Grissom, Tony Manetti, and—surprisingly—Amy Chow all were eating. "Come on in, boys," Meeker continued, "rustle yourselves some grub. Things have been downright boring around here without you." He smirked at Frank and Joe.

"Ignore him," Jamal said. They bought some burgers and onion rings and found a table as far away from Meeker as they could manage. They hung their jackets on the backs of their chairs and sat down to eat.

As they did, Amy stopped by the table. "Hey, by the way, thanks for saving my life," she said.

"All part of the service, ma'am," Joe said, pretending to tip an invisible cap to her.

"I'm surprised you're up and around so quickly," Frank said.

"When you pay for the best safety systems in the aircraft business," Amy replied, "you expect results.

Besides, I've got to find myself a new plane."

"What caused the crash?" Jamal asked.

"Multiple systems failed," Amy said. "Fuel line and avionics. I don't know how it happened, but I'm lucky to be walking. I had the plane checked before the show too. Guess I'll do my own checking from now on."

"Probably a good idea," Frank said.

"I've gotta run," she said. "I want to check out a plane demonstration. See ya. Thanks again."

"Bye," said the three boys.

"Yeah?" said a loud voice from the other side of the room. "Well, I don't think much of your business tactics either." It was Grissom, and he'd apparently been arguing with Meeker. The aging man got up from the table, slung his jacket over one shoulder, and stalked across the room.

He turned back toward Meeker halfway to the door and said, "This isn't over, hotshot." He kept walking as he talked, oblivious of where he was going.

Jamal started to move toward the two men, anticipating a fight, but he was too late. Grissom crashed into him at nearly full speed. The two of them tumbled to the floor, their jackets skidding across the faded linoleum.

Grissom turned angrily and glared at Jamal, "You want a piece of me too?" he asked, breathing into Jamal's face.

13 The Payoff

Joe and Frank rose to their feet. They crossed the room quickly and helped up their friend.

"Three against one, eh?" Grissom said. "I've faced worse odds." He assumed a defensive boxing position.

"This is just a misunderstanding," Frank said.

"Then why'd your friend trip me?" Grissom asked.

"Trip you?" Joe said angrily. "You weren't looking where you were going and ran right into him."

"Hey," Jamal said, "it's cool. It was just a mistake. You and I have no problem, Rock. Anyone who's having trouble with Meeker is a friend of mine." He leaned down and picked up his leather aviator's jacket off the floor.

Grissom grabbed his own jacket and threw it defiantly over his shoulder. "Well, just stay out of my way from now on," he said, pointing angrily at the teens. He turned quickly and stalked out the door.

"What did *he* have for lunch?" Joe said.

They finished eating and headed for the door. As they stepped outside and put on their coats, Jamal looked confused.

"What is it?" Frank asked.

"Something's in my pocket," Jamal said, pulling out a piece of crumpled paper. There were three things in the small wad: a newspaper obituary and photo, another news article, and a handwritten note in block letters. They were clipped together.

Frank peeked over Jamal's shoulder at the note. "'I have the photo. I will take it to the cops if you don't pay me what I want. Meet me tonight—you know where—or I will blow your whole scheme wide open,'" he read out loud, straight off the handwritten paper. "Jamal, do you know what this is about?"

"I've never seen any of these before," Jamal said, handing the newspaper clippings to his friends so the Hardys could examine them.

"This article is about the Carl Denny gang and the coin theft," Joe said. "It has a caption above the article, but the photo is missing. 'Captured: Beth Denny, Pablo Salvatore, John Michaelson, and Jack

117

Antonio. Gang leader Carl Denny, far right, remains at large.'"

"The obituary is for someone named Dee Jones," Frank said. "He was a machinist who died after a prolonged bout with cancer six months ago. It says his estranged wife was with him when he died. No children, apparently. I don't see any connection here to the gang, though."

"Hey, guys," Jamal said, "I don't think this is my jacket."

"What?" said Frank and Joe.

"It's not mine," Jamal said. "It *looks* like mine, but it's a bit more beat up."

"It must be Grissom's!" Joe said. "Your jackets must have gotten mixed up when he crashed into you."

"That makes sense," Jamal said. "I noticed before that his jacket and mine were practically the same."

"Put the papers back in the pocket," Frank said, looking past his friend. "Grissom's coming back." He and Joe handed the articles back to Jamal, who reclipped them to the note and stuffed the bundle into the jacket.

Grissom stalked toward them like an angry tiger. "Hey!" he called. "What did you do with my jacket?"

"What do you mean?" Jamal asked nonchalantly.

"I mean this isn't my jacket," Grissom said, taking the jacket off his shoulder and throwing it on the ground. He pointed at Jamal. "That's my jacket!"

"Really?" Frank said.

"I hadn't noticed," Jamal told Grissom.

"Give it to me!" Grissom snapped. "You didn't rifle through my pockets, did you?"

"Why would I go through your pockets?" Jamal said, acting slightly annoyed. "I told you, I didn't even notice I had the wrong jacket."

"If you'd been watching where you were going," Joe said, "this mixup would never have happened."

Grissom pulled a wallet from the jacket's pocket and flipped through it. "Well," he said, "everything *seems* to be here." He stuffed his wallet back into his jacket pocket, and turned to Frank. "Hey—just remember, keep away from my plane. I know you and your friends are mixed up in this mess somehow."

"You've been flying too high without an oxygen mask," Frank said, rolling his eyes.

"Just stay out of my way," Grissom said, stalking away.

"Well," Joe muttered as Grissom walked out of earshot, "if he meant the note for one of us, he just passed up the perfect chance to deliver it."

"So who did he intend it for?" Frank wondered. "He was arguing with Meeker in the cafeteria before."

"Amy and Manetti were there when we came in

too," Jamal noted. "Though I've got to choose Meeker as a suspect. He's caused enough trouble in my life."

"The note could be intended for someone who wasn't in the commissary," Joe said. "It was still in his pocket, after all."

"You know," Frank said, "it could be that Grissom's the one being blackmailed. Maybe he wasn't going to pass those papers to someone; maybe someone slipped the papers to him."

"We can't follow him right now," Joe said. "Whether he's the blackmailer or the victim, he'll be watching for us. We should keep an eye on him tonight, though. That's when the meeting is supposed to happen."

"How will we find the meeting place?" Jamal asked.

"Don't worry," Frank said, "I have a plan. Let's get back to the Cessna and prepare it for takeoff. We may need it tonight."

As they crossed the tarmac toward the parked Hawkins plane, they saw Rita Davenport coming in the opposite direction. She was moving quickly and waved to them as she got closer. "Have you seen Mr. Manetti?" she asked.

"He's in the cafeteria," Frank replied. "Is everything all right?"

She shook her head. "We might leave the show," she said, "especially after last night. A lot of other people are thinking about going too. Elise's trying to talk everyone into staying, but . . ." She shrugged. "There's just too much drama here. I have to run. See you later—maybe." She headed toward the cafeteria.

When the teens reached the Cessna, they discovered there were a lot fewer planes around it than there had been the previous day. Elise Flaubert, who was talking with Clevon Brooks nearby, broke off her conversation and came over to the three boys.

"You're not leaving too, are you?" she asked forlornly.

"No," Jamal said. "Not yet anyway."

"Good," she said, leaning back against the plane. "We've had such bad luck with Sullivan custom owners through this show!"

"You mean besides Jamal and Brooks?" Frank said.

"Yes," Flaubert replied, "most of the Sullivan Brothers customized planes have been damaged during the show. Two were stolen, as you know, and nearly all the rest were vandalized when Amy Chow's plane crashed."

Joe ran his hand through his hair. "A convenient crash for burglars," he said quietly.

Flaubert glanced at him and continued. "Most of the other Sullivan owners have left. There are two of these planes remaining on the airport's consignment sales block, but one was slightly damaged during Amy's crash. I doubt anyone will buy it now." She sighed. "One more thing for my insurance to handle! The other is a newer model, and not as popular. I don't think it will sell either. So, because the airport is handling sales, those two will be staying. Of active owners, only you, Brooks, and Grissom are left."

"Brooks and I have an interest in the ongoing investigation," Jamal said.

"That's true, of course," Flaubert said. "A lot of people who don't own Sullivans are talking about leaving too. Even Mr. Manetti is thinking of packing it in, and he's one of the people who convinced me to take on this show!"

"What kind of vandalization was there on the other Sullivan planes?" Frank asked, rubbing his chin. "How many did you say there were?"

"There were five others, including the two up for sale," Flaubert said. "The vandals made a terrible mess of three of them, tearing up their upholstery and paneling. Only the two for sale weren't broken into, and one of those was damaged by flying debris—the older, more valuable one, of course." She sighed again. "I was so proud to have more than a quarter of that year's Sullivan production run at the show!"

"Was anything stolen from the vandalized planes?" Frank asked.

"We're not sure yet," she replied.

"Hold on," Joe said. "You're saying that *all* the

damaged or stolen planes were from the same model year?"

"Yes," Flaubert replied. "That was a banner year for Sullivan Brothers Air Customizing. It was quite a coup to get all those planes here at the same time. I had to work really hard at convincing everyone to come. Now, of course, it's a disaster! Anyone coming to see the set will be completely disappointed.

"I'm glad Amy left her Sullivan plane at home; they're becoming extremely rare! Not that she didn't suffer enough of a loss when her plane crashed. I'm *so* glad she wasn't badly hurt," she continued. "Shoot, look at the time! I have to run, find Mitchum, and pigeonhole a few other people. But I'm *so* glad that you're not leaving. Please stay until the end of the show tomorrow."

"We will," Jamal said.

"Assuming nothing comes up," Frank added.

Flaubert sighed again. "I certainly hope nothing does! They say any publicity is good publicity, but, for airports at least, they couldn't be more wrong. See you later." She jogged off across the tarmac toward Amy, who was admiring a lime green stunt plane.

"So," Joe said, "maybe Amy's fortunes have *increased* since the crash—because her Sullivan custom is now worth more."

"Crashing a stunt plane seems like a big risk just

to increase the value of your airplane collection," Frank said.

"But she wasn't badly hurt in the crash," Jamal reminded them. "She could have set the whole thing up, either to increase her other plane's worth or as some kind of insurance scheme."

"She's not taking the loss of the *Screamin' Demon* very badly," Joe said. "That's for sure. However, if someone were pulling an insurance scam, I'd have to put my money on Brooks. We know he needs money."

Frank nodded. "Having his plane stolen might be a good way to make some easy money. But what's connecting all this to Grissom? He's either blackmailing someone or being blackmailed himself. My guess is the first, but—"

"Whoever's doing this isn't in it alone either," Joe said. "We know there were two people who hijacked Brooks's plane. We also know there were two people at the control tower last night, the one who ran from us and the one who attacked Ms. Davenport. What puzzles me is how the thieves beat us back here after shooting at us in the woods."

"Well," Frank said, "they knew where they were going, and we didn't. They still made good time, though. There could be another explanation."

"So you're pretty sure, there are more than two guys involved in this?" Jamal asked.

Frank nodded. "I'm thinking maybe it's a whole gang of people."

"The Denny gang!" Joe said. "If they're behind this, that would explain one of the articles in Grissom's pocket."

"The real question is," Frank said, "what are they after? They've broken into the administrative office, but they didn't take anything. Why were they using the control tower computer? They've stolen two planes but still came back to the airport a third time. Are they aiding someone with an insurance scam, or is it something else?" He shook his head. "I still don't really get it."

Joe shook his head. "Just once I'd like to run into a nice, simple case," he said.

"It would help if we knew what Denny and his gang looked like," Frank said. "We have to assume they've disgused themselves for this caper."

"We know Denny's done that before," Joe remarked. "Let's call Phil Cohen. He can search the Internet back in Bayport and fax us a picture or anything else he finds." Phil was a good friend of theirs, also a pro with computers.

"Good idea," Jamal said. "There's bound to be a fax in the airport office. I'll find Ms. Davenport again and ask if we can use it."

"I'll get in touch with Phil and tell him what we need," Joe said.

Frank nodded. "I'll make arrangements for following Grissom tonight and see if I can get our cell phone working again."

By the time they finished their errands and Frank repaired his cell phone, night had fallen on the air show once more. There were no further incidents during the day, and security seemed to be relaxing a bit. Mitchum could be seen poking around the airfield once more, keeping a droopy eye on things. Jose and the other field workers kept their eyes peeled as well. Despite this, many airplane owners, like Grissom, stayed close to their planes.

Tomorrow was the final day of the show, and most of the aviators were gathering for a dinner and dance in the same hangar where the opening banquet had been held. Jamal and the Hardys avoided the celebration and kept a close watch on Grissom. They made sure to stay out of clear sight.

In addition to securing the use of the airport fax, Jamal had gained clearance for a flight that evening in case they needed the plane to follow anyone Frank had rented an all-terrain Jeep as well, for any necessary ground work. They'd put the expenses on the Hawkins Air credit card.

"The cost will be worth it if we can catch these crooks and get my plane back," Jamal said.

Once the banquet was in full swing, Grissom slipped quietly into his Sullivan plane and taxied onto the runway. Jamal surreptitiously got clearance from the tower to take off right after Grissom. He and Joe planned to fly, while Frank would follow along as best he could in the Jeep. It was a tricky plan, but they couldn't be sure that Grissom might not switch to ground transportation at some point during the chase.

Grissom headed north, with the Hawkins plane following in his blind spot. Joe used Jamal's cell phone to relay information to Frank on the ground. Frank had studied maps of the area beforehand, but he still had the tricky job of tailing the planes in a Jeep.

"It looks like he's headed toward Kendall State Park," Joe said after they'd been in the air ten minutes.

"That's an awfully big area," Frank replied. "Can you give me a more specific idea of where he's going?"

"Hang on . . ." Joe said. "It looks like he's getting ready to land."

"Out here?" Jamal asked. "Where?"

Joe snapped his fingers. "Frank, remember that old farm airstrip we saw while we were searching for Jamal's plane the other day?"

"The one with the broken down barn and the rusty fuel tank near the runway?" Frank asked.

"That's the one," Joe said. "I think Grissom is landing there."

"That makes sense," Frank said. "It's close enough

to Scott Field that someone in a car could meet Grissom, but remote enough to be private. Keep on him. I'll meet you there."

Joe and Jamal watched as Grissom circled the deserted airstrip once before setting his Sullivan custom down. He taxied to the end of the small runway and stopped.

"Grissom's getting out of his plane," Joe said.

"I'm just a few minutes away," Frank called back.

Grissom walked down the runway toward the dilapidated farm house. As he passed the old fuel tank, a bright flash lit the night. The tank exploded into a huge fireball.

14 "Flight" for Life

"Frank!" Joe called. "The fuel tank just exploded!"

"Can you see Grissom?" Frank asked. "Is he okay?"

"I can't tell," Joe said. "Take us lower, Jamal."

Joe peered into the gloom and saw a dark form, the size and shape of a man, lying near the side of the airstrip. As he watched, two more dark shapes came out of the dilapidated farmhouse and moved cautiously across the grass toward the prone figure. "Grissom's down, Frank. Two guys are coming for him. Step on it!"

"I'm driving as fast as I can."

"Can you land us, Jamal?" Joe asked. "Maybe we can get there quicker than Frank."

"I can't," Jamal replied. "Grissom's plane is blocking the runway."

"Can't you come at the strip from the opposite direction?"

Jamal shook his head. "If I did, there's a good chance Frank would be scraping *us* off that runway instead of Grissom."

Joe looked out the window. "Hurry, Frank! Hurry!" he whispered.

Frank pushed the gas pedal to the floor and tore down the old gravel driveway in front of the farmhouse. Small fires in the tall grass lit the airstrip behind the house. Frank saw two masked people approaching what looked like the body of Rock Grissom.

The black-garbed figures approached cautiously at first but grew bolder when it became obvious Grissom was in no condition to fight back. They knelt to search Grissom's body and took something out of his coat. Then they stood up, and one of the people reached into his own coat, as if to draw a gun.

Frank leaned hard on the horn and flashed his headlights. He barreled full throttle straight toward the masked people. The thugs dived out of the way as Frank's Jeep rushed between them and their intended victim.

The elder Hardy hit the brakes, but couldn't stop quickly enough. The Jeep skidded across the airstrip and landed in the very tall grass on the other side.

The left-side wheels landed in a rut, and the Jeep almost tipped over. Frank spun the wheel, trying to set it right again.

Once he kicked in the four-wheel drive, the Jeep plowed up the slope through the tangled grass. As he turned the vehicle around, he saw the masked guys climbing into Grissom's airplane.

Frank spun the wheel hard and floored the gas, trying to get back to the field and cut these guys off. But the ground was very rough, and he'd made too wide a turn. As he neared the spot where Grissom lay, the stolen aircraft was already building up speed to take off.

The elder Hardy raced after them, but it was too late. Rock Grissom's stolen Sullivan Brothers aircraft soared off into the night sky.

Frank turned around and raced back to Grissom. He leaped out of the car and ran to the injured aviator's side. Grissom was unconscious and badly burned. The pupils of his eyes were dilated, and he looked as though he were slipping into shock.

A voice echoed out of the Jeep, and Frank remembered he had left his cell phone in speaker mode resting on the seat of the car. "Don't worry, Frank," Joe's voice said. "We're on them. They won't get away from us."

Frank dashed back to the Jeep and picked up the phone. "Never mind the thieves," Frank said. "I need you down here. Grissom's in really bad shape.

We need to get him to a hospital, pronto. The car may not be fast enough."

"But the thieves will get away!" Jamal interjected.

"We'll have to let them go again," Frank said. "Grissom knows who they are anyway. I'll bet he'll testify against them—*if* he lives through this. Check their heading before you land. I have a feeling I may know where those guys are going."

"Get the car off the runway, Frank," Joe said. "We're coming down."

Frank moved the Jeep away from the airstrip, and less than two minutes later, the Hawkins Air Cessna was on the ground. Jamal taxied over to Grissom, while Frank did what he could for the aviator's injuries. Then Frank and Joe loaded the wounded man into the back of the plane.

"I called ahead to the airstrip," Jamal said. "They'll have an ambulance waiting when I get there."

"Good," Frank said. "I've done my best to stabilize him. If you can take care of Grissom, Joe and I will go after the thieves. What was their heading last time you saw them?"

"North by northwest," Jamal said.

Joe whistled. "Straight toward Lake Kendall."

"Keep the cell phone connection open as long as you can," Frank said to Jamal. "Come on, Joe." The brothers closed and secured the doors to the Cessna, then hopped into the Jeep.

As Jamal's airplane lifted into the air, the Hardys

got into the Jeep and tore down the old farm road toward the highway.

"I didn't see anyone driving away when I arrived," Frank said. "The thieves must have been dropped off earlier and waited for Grissom."

"That means at least three guys are working together on this," Joe said. "Unless they took a taxi."

"And left a witness?" Frank said. "I doubt it. Besides, we know there are five people in the Denny gang—if it's them. See if you can find a way around Lake Kendall on the map. There must be one, or the thieves wouldn't be able to get between their hideout and the airport so quickly."

"You're thinking they're in that rusty barn we saw by the lake," Joe said.

Frank nodded. "What we thought were snowmobile tracks on the lake were actually airplane tracks. We assumed that the criminals had just touched down to pick up the parachutist you fought with and then left again. But what if they meant to land on the lake all the time?" He screeched the Jeep off the dirt road and onto the highway heading toward Kendall State Park.

"I get it," Joe said. "The tracks were there because they'd done it before—at least once."

"That's where they took Jamal's Sullivan Brothers plane," Frank said, "and Brooks's plane too. We didn't see it land because we were too busy trying not to get killed in the skydiving accident."

"So you think they're taking Grissom's plane there as well," Joe said.

Frank nodded. "We know Carl Denny either crashed eight-seven-eight into the lake or dumped it there deliberately."

"That would mean he had knowledge of the area," Joe said, "and you can't miss that old metal barn. That would explain why the sniper chased us for so long. He was trying to make sure we didn't find their hideout." He pointed to a side road coming up. "Turn right here."

Frank turned the car onto the side road but kept his foot firmly on the gas. "But why is Denny trying to steal these planes now? His old gang went to jail for five years, but he's been out. Why steal these planes now? What's he want?"

They drove in silence awhile as both pondered these questions. The cell phone's ring broke the silence. It was Jamal.

"I just got in," he said. "The EMTs are working on Grissom, but a fax came from Phil Cohen while we were gone. It's a picture of Carl Denny."

"Great," Joe said. "Which one of the people at the show is he?"

"That's just it," Jamal said. "He's not any of the people we were wondering about; he's the guy in the obituary from Grissom's pocket. Carl Denny is dead."

The brothers sat in stunned silence for a moment.

Frank pulled them onto the road leading around Lake Kendall to the northeast shore, where they'd seen the old barn.

"But if Denny is dead, who's pulling these jobs?" Joe asked.

Frank looked puzzled a moment and then laughed. "Think about it a minute, Joe," he said. "Denny's being dead makes perfect sense."

A smile slowly crept across Joe Hardy's face. "You're right, Frank," he said. "The date on that obituary was six months ago. That explains why these crimes are happening now—as well as the trouble with this particular set of Sullivan Brothers planes."

"Well, I don't get it," Jamal said, his voice echoing over the speakerphone.

"Has Phil found a photo of the gang yet, Jamal?" Frank asked.

"No," Jamal replied. "Not yet."

"Call Phil and tell him it's imperative that he find that photo," Joe said. "And ask him to find out when the Denny gang got out on parole. I'm betting it's just over six months ago."

"So the Denny gang, minus Denny, is behind all this?" Jamal asked.

"That's our guess," Frank said.

"What did you say?" Jamal replied. "You're break . . . up!"

Joe hung up the phone. "We've lost the cell connection again."

"That means we're getting close to where we parachuted down. Take the next trail on the left. If I'm reading this map right, we're driving to the back of the barn."

"Just let me know when to kill the headlights," Frank said. "We already know these guys have guns, and I'd rather they didn't see us coming."

A few minutes later they turned off the car's lights and drove in the dark up the final curve to the warehouse. Frank stopped a short distance away. Joe tucked the cell phone into his pocket. They got out and moved cautiously through the woods up to the old barn.

The structure was as large as an air hangar. It had big metal doors on either end and a smaller door on one side near the back. The old farm building close to the barn had long fallen into ruin, though enough of its white columns remained to give an impression of its former glory. A row of airplane tracks led up from the frozen lake and stopped at the big doors on the lakeward side. The building had only a few small translucent windows. Dim light leaked out from behind them.

Joe and Frank crept up to the side of the building. They listened but heard no noise from inside. Trying to see through the windows without being seen was impossible even if they weren't totally transparent, so the brothers cautiously moved to the small door near the back. Frank checked it; it was unlocked.

They slowly opened the door and slipped inside.

The interior of the old barn smelled like a machine shop. Smells of oil, metal, electricity, and fuel filled the stuffy air. Large piles of junk lay near the door: spare parts from machines, both old and new. Three huge airplanes practically filled the room. The brothers immediately recognized the Sullivan Brothers custom planes owned by Hawkins Air, Clevon Brooks, and—the most recent arrival— Dale "Rock" Grissom.

Scattered about the floor lay the carefully crafted interiors of the Sullivan planes. The Hawkins Air plane was facing the door where the brothers came in. The Brooks plane was in the middle of the hangar, and the Grissom plane stood near the big doors on the lakeward side.

"See anyone?" Frank whispered.

"No," Joe whispered back. "Let's look around. Obviously, we're in the right place."

As the brothers stepped forward, the stolen plane's engine started, and its big prop spun to life. The plane lurched forward, and the propeller bore in on the brothers, threatening to cut the Hardys to pieces.

15 Flying Finish

The wind from the prop of Jamal's dad's stolen plane forced the brothers back. The deafening roar of its engine filled their ears. The plane rolled toward Frank and Joe, its deadly propeller a blur in the barn's dim light.

The Hardys backed into the junk piled by the door, and scrap metal rained down on them. They couldn't retreat any further. They were trapped.

"Down!" yelled Frank.

He and Joe dived to either side of the propeller, and it just passed over their heads. The boys rolled as they hit the floor, then quickly got to their feet again. As they did, Joe spotted a man in a black mask holding a rifle aimed directly at Frank.

Joe pulled the cell phone out of his pocket and

heaved it at the gunman. The sniper fired, but Joe's impromptu missile hit him hard as he pulled the trigger. The cell phone smashed into pieces, but the shot went awry, missing Frank.

Frank charged forward and grabbed the gunman before he could fire again. The two of them wrestled for a moment, Frank pinning the barrel against the masked man's chest. The man facing him was bigger and heavier than Frank. He began to force the teenager back toward the hangar wall.

Joe rushed to the plane cockpit's door just as the second masked man piloting Brooks's plane tried to get out. The younger Hardy hit the hatch hard, smashing the door into the thief's chest and arm. The man yelped and staggered forward. Joe grabbed him by the shirt and punched him square in the face. The man fell backward and hit his head against the fuselage of Jamal's stolen plane. He slumped to the floor, unconscious.

The gunman kept pushing Frank toward the wall. Out of the corner of his eye, Frank saw several big workbenches piled with rusty tools. They were right behind him. If the gunman pushed Frank into one of them, he wouldn't have to fire a shot; he could either break Frank's back against the table or strangle him by pressing the stock of the gun into his neck.

Frank threw himself backward onto the floor, pushing the gunman over him as he fell. The throw worked. Frank let go of the gun, and the sniper sailed past him and smashed hard into a heavy workbench. The gunman groaned and tried to swing the gun around, but Frank sprang to his feet and kicked the man in the side of the head.

The sniper hit the floor like a sack of potatoes and didn't move. Frank went to help Joe and saw his brother already coming to *his* aid. "Let's tie these guys up and find out who they are," Frank said.

The brothers scrounged some rope from the piles of junk and quickly had the thieves securely trussed. Then they pulled off the felons' masks.

"Mitchum and Jose," Frank said, hardly surprised.

"Or, more accurately, Pablo Salvatore and John Michaelson, half of the remaining Carl Denny gang," Joe said. "They must have heard us coming. Good thing they weren't better prepared."

"Mitchum wasn't a very good shot anyway," Frank said. "He missed us plenty of times in the forest." Mitchum scowled back at Frank.

"He wasn't a very good security guard either," Joe said. "I think Flaubert may need to find another."

"And a new maintenance man too," Frank added, looking at Jose. "No wonder Scott Field is such a wreck. Let's see if these guys found what they were looking for."

The brothers stowed the thieves in the storage compartment of Brooks's plane. They spent the next few minutes searching through the hangar, but found no sign of the missing coins. "Nothing," Joe said.

"I guessed as much," Frank replied. "If they'd found them, they would have stopped searching. Carl Denny must have died before he could tell the rest of the gang exactly where he hid the coins."

Joe nodded. "He probably stashed the money when he was working at the Sullivan Brothers customizing shop. Since he was working on airplanes, it would be easy to hide some rare coins in the paneling or upholstery. Plus an airplane makes a great escape vehicle."

"I think if we check," Frank said, "we'll find that all the planes that have been ransacked during the air show were in the Sullivan Brothers custom shop on the night Denny made his big escape."

"So, in the confusion of the police chase, Denny escaped in the wrong plane," Joe said. "That makes sense. The planes were probably all painted fairly similarly at the time since they weren't finished. But if the stolen coins aren't here . . ."

"There's only one place they can be," Frank said. "We need to get back to Scott Field before someone in the gang does."

"The Jeep may not be fast enough," Joe said. "Which plane should we take?"

"Grissom's is our best bet," Frank said. "It hasn't been here long enough for them to chop it up too badly. Open the barn doors while I start it up."

He hurried over to the Grissom plane and

jumped in. Joe opened the big doors out onto the lake and then climbed into the copilot's seat.

"They've ripped out the radio," Frank said, "but the rest of the control panel is still good. I think we can fly it."

Joe nodded. "Let's roll!"

Frank taxied the slightly beaten-up Sullivan plane out onto the lake and, following the tracks laid down in the thin snow by the planes that had been stolen and hidden, executed a perfect takeoff.

"Whew!" he said. "Don't ask me to do that again."

"All you have to worry about now," Joe replied, "is getting us to Scott Field before the other thieves get away."

They headed south southeast toward the air show.

"Hey," Joe said, picking something out the ashtray near the center of the control panel, "Here's the picture from that newspaper article Grissom was using as blackmail. He must have stashed it here for safe keeping."

"Are the remaining members of the gang who we think they are?" Frank asked.

"Yep," Joe replied.

"Too bad you smashed our cell phone," Frank said, "or we could call ahead and alert the cops."

"Which would you rather have, a smashed cell phone or a shot in the head?" Joe asked.

"You made the right choice," Frank said with a smile.

As they arrived back at Scott Field, they saw another plane on the tarmac that was heading for the runway.

"The last scratched-up Sullivan custom," Joe said, "straight from the consignment block. Any bets who's in the pilot seat?"

"Hang on," Frank said. "I'm going to bring us in low and fast."

Frank banked their borrowed aircraft low over the control tower, just to get the authorities' attention. Then he made a sharp turn and brought the plane on the runway. He taxied to a stop right in front of the final Sullivan custom plane, blocking its takeoff.

He and Joe hopped out onto the tarmac as police sirens wailed, toward them. Flaubert and other air officials ran out onto the field with Jamal in tow.

A very angry man climbed out of the blocked plane's cockpit and raised his hands up in irritation. "What right do you have to do this?" he asked. "We could have been hurt!"

"Not half the menace you are, Mr. Manetti," Joe said. "You've stolen planes and sabotaged this whole air show."

"That's absurd," Manetti said. "I've just bought this plane! Now get out of my way. I've had enough shenanigans at this convention."

"You had to buy it," Frank said. "With Mitchum and Jose tied up in Kendall State Park, you had no chance of stealing a fourth plane."

"You and the rest of Carl Denny's gang are behind all the trouble at the Fly By & Buy," Joe said, "and we've got the picture to prove it."

As the police, airport security, the NTSB agent, Elise Flaubert, and Jamal closed in, Joe held out the picture of the Denny gang from the newspaper article.

"I think you'll recognize four of those people, Ms. Flaubert," Joe said. "After all, two of them worked for you."

"You might as well come out too, Ms. Davenport—or should I say Mrs. Beth Denny," Frank said to a figure still lurking in the cockpit of the final Sullivan plane. "Seems you're *grounded*!"

By the following morning, the police and aviation officials had rounded up the rest of the Denny gang and locked them all in jail. The local authorities took credit for capturing the criminals, and this was fine with the Hardys. The brothers were used to being left out of the spotlight, and frankly, they preferred it that way.

Just before noon Amy Chow took the brothers and Jamal out to brunch, to thank them for catching the criminals who had sabotaged her plane.

"So, the old Carl Denny gang was behind all of the trouble at the Fly By & Buy?" Amy asked.

"Yep," Joe replied. "They got caught during the big coin robbery, but Denny got away. He stashed the loot in an airplane at Sullivan Brothers when he worked there. But when the police nearly caught him, he took off in the wrong plane."

"He probably spent the rest of his life searching for the coins," Frank said. "If we check some old news stories, we might even find a trail of Sullivan plane vandalism leading back to him."

"But he died of cancer before he found the stolen coins," Jamal said. "Man, is that ironic!"

Joe nodded. "As the fax Phil sent last night confirmed," he said, "the rest of the gang was in prison until a few months ago. When they got out, Denny's wife tracked him down. He was dying at that point, but he managed to tell Rita, or should I say Beth, that he'd stashed the coins in one of the Sullivan Brothers planes that were in the shop the night he escaped."

"He couldn't tell her which one, though," Frank continued. "The planes have all changed hands and been repainted a couple of times since. The one that looked closest to the plane Denny stole— eight-seven-eight—was Jamal's plane. That's why the gang stole Jamal's plane first."

"Lucky me!" Jamal said, a hint of sarcasm in his voice.

"It was lucky for the thieves that all those Sullivan planes were here at the show together," Chow said.

"Not lucky at all," Frank replied. "Scott Field was in bad financial shape. Flaubert was grasping at straws to keep the airport afloat. She told us that Tony Manetti suggested that she bring the planes to the show. Remembering that tipped us off to Manetti's ties with the criminals behind the trouble."

"So Manetti set this whole scheme up?" Jamal said.

"With Davenport," Joe said, nodding. "They were the brains behind the operation, though Manetti brought plenty of brawn too."

"It was Manetti who broke into the administration office and the control tower," Frank said. "The gang needed the show registration papers to figure out which of the Sullivan planes were from the group Denny worked on. Jose helped Manetti escape us that time. He misdirected us so that we wouldn't catch his boss."

"Rita Davenport covered up for Manetti during the control tower break-in," added Joe. "That time they were trying to use the tower computer to cover up the flight paths they'd taken when stealing the planes. Davenport screamed that night to keep us from catching Manetti."

"So the attack on her was completely fake?" Jamal asked.

"Exactly," Joe replied. "The thieves had their scheme well coordinated; they made sure they could cover for one another. Mitchum was the pilot who flew Brooks's stolen plane out to Kendall State Park. He'd put in a long shift the day before, and no one at the airport expected him back that day. Jose overpowered Brooks, then went with Mitchum to help strip the plane down once they reached the old barn."

"But neither of them counted on your pulling Jose out of that plane," Jamal said.

"No, but my interference didn't slow them down very much," Joe said. "Jose hooked up with Mitchum at the barn, and they came after Frank and me. They only managed to chase us into the river."

"Having Mitchum as the field's main security guard and Jose working as a janitor was a huge help to this operation," Frank said. "The gang had been planning this for a long time—long enough to get two people working inside the airport."

Amy shook her head. "They played Elise Flaubert like a violin."

"I feel bad for her," Jamal said. "This might end her career."

"Let's hope not," Frank said.

"She doesn't deserve it," Joe added. "This was a very slick operation."

"No wonder this case was so hard to solve," Jamal said. "Every time we thought we had one of the thieves pegged another would appear."

"Well, no matter what the media say, I'll still know who saved the day," Amy said. She raised her glass of orange juice in a toast. "I heard they recovered the stolen coins from that last plane this morning."

"It was just bad luck that the thieves chose the right plane last," Frank said. "If they'd discovered the coins earlier, we might never have caught them. They would have probably taken their money and run."

"I hope the reward from the recovery will pay for the damages to Jamal's plane and the other victims' losses," Joe said.

"If it doesn't," Amy said, "maybe I'll set up a charitable fund to cover the difference."

Jamal smiled at Amy. "I *knew* there was a reason I liked you," he said.

She laughed. "And if there's anything I can do for you, Frank and Joe," she said, "just let me know. Without you the criminals might have flown the coop."

"Yeah," Joe replied. "Good thing their wings are now clipped!"

Get spooked *with this other Cassie Hartt mystery!*

On a cruise to the Caribbean, fourteen-year-old Cassie Hartt hopes to reconnect with her father, who she hasn't seen since her parents' divorce. But spending time with her new stepmother and stepsister leaves her feeling like an outsider. So she's thrilled when she meets Charles. Not only is he a cute boy her own age, but he's on a mysterious mission.

Charles is headed to Martinique to find an ancient silver statue that may be the cause of a curse in his family. Cassie can't resist a good mystery, so she decides to team up with Charles. But they aren't the only ones looking for the statue—and the other interested parties will stop at nothing to get their hands on it....

Test your detective skills with these spine-tingling Aladdin Mysteries!

The Star-Spangled Secret
By K. M. Kimball

Secret of the Red Flame
By K. M. Kimball

Scared Stiff
By Willo Davis Roberts

O'Dwyer & Grady
Starring in Acting Innocent
By Eileen Heyes

Ghosts in the Gallery
By Barbara Brooks Wallace

The York Trilogy By Phyllis Reynolds Naylor

Shadows on the Wall

Faces in the Water

Footprints at the Window

Follow the *Scrappers* on their quest for the championship in the action-packed new baseball series from Aladdin Paperbacks and Atheneum Books for Young Readers

Scrappers #1
Will Robbie's ego destroy his chance to play ball?
PLAY BALL!
SCRAPPERS
FREE! Trivia Trading Cards
DEAN HUGHES

Scrappers #2
What's happened to Wilson's long ball?
HOME RUN HERO

Scrappers #3
Could Trent be jealous of his best friend?
TEAM PLAYER
SCRAPPERS
FREE! Trivia Trading Cards
DEAN HUGHES

coming in April

Simon & Schuster Children's Publishing Division